KNOWLEDGE AFORETHOUGHT

ON BEHALF OF DEATH, BOOK 2

E.G. STONE

TARNEY BRAE CREATIVE ENDEAVOURS

For my fellow time travellers

CONTENTS

TIME IS RELATIVE

"You should wear this, Cal," my assistant said, holding up a black silk cummerbund like it hadn't gone out of style twenty years ago. Yolanda was grinning widely, her strangely white teeth contrasting sharply with her rock troll features: bald, with greyish-green skin that was tough as elephant hide, a squat nose and big yellowy eyes. She was also about the size of an American football running-back. Basically: scary, dangerous, and far too keen on my fashion choices. Granted, she was a whizz at computers and knew the ins and outs of every social media platform from the mortal realms to Elsewhere. And, despite the addiction to salt—apparently it was a rock troll thing—she was extremely reliable. She sat in the extra large leather chair at her desk, spinning back and forth and looking like a kid at Christmas. I narrowed my eyes and pushed my glasses up.

"You should maybe stop raiding the thrift store every time we go into the mortal realms," I retorted.

My other employee, Agravaine, snorted. He was an air elemental that had been kicked out (or escaped from, depending on who you ask) The Order of Silence after I got involved and nearly died, and instead came to work with me as an assisting marketing agent. So far, he had scared more clients away than he had brought in. Oddly, that was a far more helpful trait than I had anticipated, even if it meant all the marketing was on my shoulders. He closed the lid of his laptop and leaned back in his chair, propping his feet on his desk, opposite the room from Yolanda.

"That's like trying to get her to give up salted foods," Agravaine said. He winked at Yolanda when she gaped in horror at the mere thought and I smothered the urge to roll my eyes. Agravaine was the sort of classically handsome person that got people to like him just by smiling. It was extremely useful for building up an online presence. It was also extremely annoying to someone like me—that is to say, a perfectly ordinary human in a world of magical beings—who got ignored whenever he was around. Of course, neither he nor Yolanda liked to be around when it came to dealing with our primary client and my boss. They were downright terrified. Me? I was more...respectful by necessity.

To be fair, most people didn't like being around when it came to our boss. That was why I had been hired in the first place. He had brought me from the mortal realms—just as I was being shot, which was not a great time—to Elsewhere to head up a marketing and PR firm to improve his image.

Granted, that new job then immediately required I go solve a murder, got me mostly-dead on more than one occasion, and now resulted in my participation as chaperone…

My name is Cal Thorpe. I work for Death. And I was stupid enough to start this job without a proper job description.

"While I'm gone, would someone please tell Doc Graveltoes to stop posting selfies with his patients while they're unconscious? It's a little creepy," I said to Yolanda, doing my best to tuck in my shirt without wrinkling it.

"Okay, Cal," Yolanda said cheerfully, typing the note into her computer. Agravaine just snorted. Again.

"It's your own fault for getting him a cell phone anyways," he said. "Why would you give a phone to a gremlin? And then teach him how to use it?"

"I just want to do marketing. Okay? Marketing. If that means getting phones to gremlins or setting up interviews with people who are cultishly pleased to be talking with Death, so be it. But *this*? I have to chaperone Life and Death to the theatre!"

"Death is in charge," Yolanda breathed like I had just renounced all salted foods for the rest of my life. She wasn't wrong, but that didn't make me like it any more.

"Babysitting two supernatural entities that could blow up the world with a sneeze isn't in my job description," I grumbled, messing with my bowtie.

"Well, at least you get good benefits," Yolanda chimed in, flashing her too-white teeth with that annoyingly cheerful grin. I scowled deeper.

"Yeah," Agravaine snickered, stretching and fixing me with a smug grin. "They're to die for."

"I was wrong. Babysitting those two will be a picnic compared to dealing with the two of you."

I huffed and reached down to tie my shoe and polish the leather surface a touch. I will say one thing about working for Death: despite the job risks I have inadvertently walked into, he pays very well. Enough to buy the high-end shoes for this ridiculous night out. Why couldn't a night out in New York City for me include just wandering around and eating a hot dog or going to a nice restaurant? Why did it have to include chaperoning Death and his completely-insane wife, Life, to the theatre? I had complained over and over again that I wasn't a relationship counsellor, but no one seemed to take me seriously.

I straightened, grumbled, shoved my fully-charged phone in my pocket and grabbed my blazer. "Might as well get this over with. I hope I don't get blown to smithereens, or eaten by a wyvern, or kidnapped by vampires. Again."

"Good luck!" Yolanda called as I trudged to the office door. I waved over my shoulder, not entirely unhappy to be leaving my perpetually cheerful assistant behind. Especially as I heard, "So, how long do you think they'll make it this time?" behind my back as I left. I winced.

"Twenty minutes," Agravaine replied.

"Fifty bucks says you're wrong," Yolanda said.

"Done."

I really needed a vacation. A *normal* vacation.

ADVICE TO ANYONE starting out on a new job: I would suggest getting a very thorough job description before you begin. Otherwise, you will end up much like myself, doing things that you did not expect under the wildest of circumstances. Granted, my situation is a little bit more unusual than otherwise, but the principle still holds. See, for me, everything started to go sideways when I was just about to be promoted to vice president of my marketing firm. I was moving up in the world. I had people begging me to take them on as clients. I had the nod from the owner of the firm, Old lady Harcourt. Then, as I was walking to a lovely dinner where I anticipated the most wonderful promotion after working quite hard, I encountered Death.

Death, as it turns out, is actually a rather nice guy. He is tall, gaunt, with skin darker than the shadows themselves—in fact, he seems to create them—and instead of eyes he has nothing but empty holes that will swallow you, er, alive if you look too long. But apart from the fact that he is perhaps one of the most terrifying things I have ever encountered, Death is actually a nice guy. I met him on a park bench after being shot. He was wearing a three-piece suit, explained the not-so-good position I was in, and then, he offered me a job. He offered me a job. I was to be his new public relations manager. Given that my options just then were quite painful and completely unknown, I closed my eyes, shook his hand, and accepted.

The results were...unexpected.

Now, almost a year later, I was working way outside my usual job parameters of marketing and public relations. I was acting as chaperone and relationship counsellor to Life and Death, hoping to smooth out some of the wrinkles in their marriage. As you might expect, they have some serious wrinkles. And no, the wrinkles were not my fault. Entirely.

On this particular night, I was playing chaperone to Life and Death on a foray into the mortal realm, where we would be going to a decently posh theatre, surrounded by perfectly normal people, and watching *The Mikado.* I figured that some Gilbert and Sullivan would do us all well. I mean, it's hard to start an argument when you have people singing and dancing in front of you. And blowing up a building in front of mortals was a serious taboo, so I figured we'd be safe. Ish.

It would definitely be a better option than the morose tea party at The Order of Silence we attended the week before. That had nearly resulted in the literal liquidation of a whole lot of people, including myself. The Order of Silence was still trying to stick me with the bill for damages. Then there was sandwiches at the tavern just on the border of Life's lands and Death's territory in Elsewhere. I, at least, had the foresight to order my reuben to go.

This time, I figured that they would *have* to behave since we were going to be wandering around with a bunch of very fragile, very innocent, very ignorant humans. No magic. No destruction. Nada.

That, and it was Gilbert and Sullivan. If they liked

it, then they had something to talk about. If they hated it, then they had something to talk about. Either way, I would be out of Elsewhere and into the mortal realms and doing my very best to deal with headache. There would be no magic, no people trying to kill me. I could pretend that I was just a normal guy, accompanying his boss and boss' wife to the theatre. It would almost be like it was.

Not that appearing out of thin air in the park across the street from the theatre was anything remotely approaching normal. At least I didn't throw up.

As we were going to one of the more upscale features in my former hometown of a very large city, we were dressed to the nines. Death had worn the guise of a very tall black man who looked like he could play basketball for any of the teams the world and perhaps make a very large and tidy fortune. He wore, as usual, a three-piece suit, and looked quite dapper. Life hadn't bothered with such nonsense as a guise. She went as herself; that is to say, I couldn't tell you whether or not she was tall or short, thin or curvy, only that she was absolutely stunning in every way. She wore some sort of cocktail dress in a shimmery fabric. I was uncertain of the colour, simply because I had a hard time looking away from her long enough to notice something as mundane as her clothes. She was drawing the attention of everyone she passed as we walked into the theatre.

I, being human and not nearly so good at being noticed, looked completely boring by comparison to these two. I wore a nice pair of trousers and a button up shirt and some shiny loafers. I had put on my very best pair of glasses, the ones with the thick black frames, and even managed to tame my wavy brown hair into some semblance of order. Still, compared to Life and Death, I was pretty ordinary.

"I don't mean to be…difficult," I said as we shoved our way past some people at the drinks bar, "but wouldn't it have been a little bit better to try and blend into the mortal realms?"

Life looked at me as though I were nothing but a bug beneath her very pointy shoes. "Cal," she said. "You know nothing of humans, despite the fact that you are one. An interesting phenomenon, but the fact remains. Humans will see what they wish to see. Even now, they are coming up with some picture in their mind of what exactly I am. All they know is that I am exactly what they want. What should it matter to me what I look like?"

"Because my dear," Death said, walking on the other side of me and doing his very best not to grind his teeth, "we are trying to maintain a low profile. It is difficult to do so when you choose to walk around as yourself. More and more people are capable of seeing that which we would not wish them to see. It is one of the few benefits of having such technology at their disposal. Besides, we are meant to be here to enjoy the performance, not participate in one."

Life scoffed, tossed her head, and strode off, sashaying her hips as she went. As I stood next to Death, part of me desperately wanted to fall in after her. She was *Life*. Tempting, wonderful, bright, beautiful. But, I knew Life and she was not as pleasant as one would think. She was in fact rather difficult. Fickle. Cruel. Unfair. Uncaring. Death on the other hand, while terrifying, was at least sane.

"You know, I'm only your public relations and marketing manager," I said, not for the first time, not even for the first time that evening. "Perhaps it would be better if someone else did this for you. Mercy for instance? Or even Yolanda."

Mercy was an air elemental like Agravaine who worked for The Order of Silence, a group of assassins and zealots dedicated to maintaining a balance between Life and Death. The Order and I weren't on the best of terms after I had liberated Agravaine and failed to die properly. Mercy, being their liaison with Death, did her best to avoid me as much as possible. She hated Yolanda, Agravaine and myself for bringing about the death of her sometimes associate Justice the year before. It was—truly—not my fault, but every interaction since had ended up with me desperately wishing to be far, far away.

"Mercy would live up to her name, which is not what Life, or myself, need. She cannot help being merciful. We cannot help needing anything but mercy. And Yolanda is, understandably, terrified of us both. Besides, she has a harder time fitting into the mortal realms than you do, Cal. Nor do you seem to be deferentially terrified of us. A human trait, I imagine. No, you are just going to have to accept that this is the necessary course of action. We must sort this out between us, or things are going to get a whole lot worse."

Death followed after his wayward wife and I paused a moment, trying to think how things could really become much worse. Given my experience with the magical and supernatural world, I decided there were many many ways that could be managed. So I shoved my hands into my pockets, touched my phone to reassure myself that there would still be the constants of technology and social media in these mad times, and walked after my charges, hoping that this night could at least be maintained without the yelling of our last two sessions. I didn't have the legal capacity to battle more demands for payments for damages.

The viewing box from which we were going to watch *The Mikado* was understandably grandiose. The chairs were plush and lined with velvet, the exposed wood was gilded, the walls were carved into fantastical shapes, and the balcony was in full view of the entire theatre. I wasn't surprised. After all, the point of these old theatres was to be a place where you could be seen. I only hoped that we could be seen without causing a scene.

There were four plush chairs in the box, three of which were taken up by Life, myself, and Death. I hoped that the fourth chair would be empty, or used by someone who was aware of the situation, otherwise the evening would be incredibly and increasingly awkward. How do you explain to a human—especially a truly mortal one, instead of the immortal and enlightened sort that I was these days—about the whole relationship counselling between Life and Death issue? These were some of the most powerful beings in the universe, and they could probably level the average human with a good glare. I had been given various assurances that this would all go well, but we all know the value of good intentions.

Life fanned herself with the brochures for the musical, staring at the filling theatre with interest. Each time her gaze focused on a particular person, they seemed to become more animated, more vibrant. When she looked away, they slumped as if exhausted. Death flipped through the pages almost mechanically, casually glancing over the advertisements and articles and descriptions of the actors' roles. He ignored Life's bored antics. I sat between them and twirled my phone in my hand though I didn't use it, trying not to think of impending doom. I pushed up the glasses on my nose, and then blessed relief, the lights flashed twice to indicate the start of the performance.

During the performance itself, Life and Death behaved themselves...generally speaking. One thing I hadn't considered was that they would like certain parts of the show that the other didn't like. Death particularly appreciated the bit about a list of potential victims. Life particularly appreciated all of the other pieces about tricking Death. As far as I could tell, they were just relegating themselves to glaring at each other out of the corners of their eyes. So far so good. I tried to pay attention to the performance and got almost nowhere. I was a little worried about my charges accidentally blowing up the theatre with me in it. Then—finally—intermission.

"I'm getting some drinks," I said as soon as the lights went up. Life flicked her brows up with interest. Death waved a hand in acknowledgement.

"Nothing for me, thank you Cal. We will be perfectly fine in your absence," Death assured me. I narrowed my eyes.

"Five minutes," I said. "It took five minutes for the whole tavern too—"

"I will behave if you hurry and bring me a drink!" Life snapped. I was tempted to chew her out, too, but I dutifully trudged away to the nearest bar. People gave me looks at my unmoving scowl, but stayed out of my way. Mostly.

There seemed to be some sort of magic surrounding the bars in the theatre during intermission, so I barely managed to squeak out three glasses of wine before the two minute mark when the show would start again. I returned to the box, balancing the drinks precariously and cursing every cheerful show goer that stood in my way. Did they *want* to die?

Thankfully, the theatre was still standing when I returned to the box. There was no shouting, no pitched battle, and the audience hadn't burst into screaming panic. My blood pressure dropped minutely. Life and Death hadn't managed to level the theatre or kill each other, so I took the win. However, there was a third person now in the box.

He was tall, though not as tall as Death, and had a sort of casual air about him, as though he had seen everything, done everything, and still enjoyed causing trouble. He didn't seem to be dark or light, weak or strong, he just sort of was, in the way that the earth beneath your feet is, or the way the stars in the sky are. He was. Despite this gravitas, his shoulders were artfully slouched and he wore a modern, expensive, and wrinkled suit. He stuck one hand into his pocket and grabbed a glass of wine from my hand with the other. Life snatched the remaining glass, leaving me with nothing. Perhaps it was a good thing, considering.

"Well, well," the stranger said looking me over like a new toy. "Interesting. I have met many immortals in my time, but never a human one. Life, darling, what did you do? This is the latest of your playthings?" The stranger spoke with a sort of drawl, though he had a relatively British accent. I wasn't quite sure I like the way he smirked at me.

Life looked at me and curled her lips. "He is not mine. Death refuses to let me play with him."

"The only reason that you didn't burn me to a crisp, lady, is the fact that Death made a mistake when extending my life," I snapped. Life shrugged, and turned back to watch the crowd from the box.

"Time," Death said nodding to be stranger, "this is Cal Thorpe. He is my public relations manager and marketing expert. He is also acting as mediator between Life and myself."

I would have choked, had I been drinking wine, but it had been taken by the other beings in the box. Instead, I coughed into my hand. "Time? You're Time?"

The immensely powerful being nodded casually

and stretched out his hand for me to shake. I took it rather hesitantly—since Death had fixed my unfortunate inability to be killed at all, I tried to avoid having contact with beings who were dangerous enough to destroy by touch. That included Life and Death. Time, despite having a serious presence, seemed to just be a perfectly normal being. At least, I didn't feel any pain or terror or rapid ageing or anything while shaking Time's hand.

"Yes," Time said. He took a sip of his wine and tucked his spare hand back into his pocket. "Death is my cousin. We see each other now and again, when certain forces align."

I winced. Neither Death nor Life looked terribly concerned by this statement, but I had been introduced to the world of magic and mayhem rather more spectacularly than otherwise. One of the first things I learned was to be wary when people made statements like that. "And what forces aligned to bring you here today?" I asked before I could consider whether or not my words would be rude. I needn't have worried.

"You needn't look so glum, little human. You act as though escorting my cousin and his effervescent wife to the theatre is a burden, not the wonderment it should be. Not many have the opportunities you have, even before their time expires."

"Yes, well, excuse me if I have to worry about a city block being levelled a whole lot more now than I did when I was just an ordinary 'little' human."

Time just chuckled and sank into the spare chair as

the lights flashed, indicating that the second half of the performance was about to begin.

I settled back into my chair between the feuding Life and Death and really hoped that the remainder of the night wouldn't go badly. The stress of the situation was going to give me an ulcer. And now *Time* was showing up? I rubbed my sternum, certain that I was going to have an acid reflux attack.

I shouldn't have bothered with all the worrying; things seem to often go badly without my input at all.

As far as performances went, the second half of the show was as expected. Gilbert and Sullivan shows being ridiculous, this was that and more. Life and Death seemed suitably distracted from their disagreements with each other to relax a little bit. Time seemed more interested in watching me. I knew this because I could feel him staring at the back of my head. But as soon as I would turn around to look, his eyes would be fixed elsewhere, although never actually on the performance. By the time the show was over, I was feeling extremely jumpy.

The cast came out for bows, smiling as though they had no cares in the world. I envied them, the ignorant, normal, fragile humans. I pushed up my glasses on my nose again, before standing and clapping with the rest of the people in the audience. Death gave an appropriately polite smattering of applause. Life didn't even bother, she just lounged languidly in her chair. The normal people started filtering out of the theatre.

"Are we quite done with this nonsense?" Life asked.

"I have a few things to tend to, which are rather more important than this outing."

"Things to tend to?" Death asked, a hint of iron in his voice. I took a deep breath, tried to remember the zen teachings from my yoga studio back when I was a living being, and prepared to face off between two battling beings. "That wouldn't include trying to expand your territory in Elsewhere again? I've noticed a few of your particular favourites gathering along the edge of my territory."

"You're being paranoid," Life said with a dismissive wave of her hand. "Why would I want your realm?"

Death started to speak and I decided that it was perhaps time to intervene. "That was a really good show," I said loudly. Life looked at me as though I had shoved something particularly nasty in her face. Death just let out a low breath and pinched the bridge of his nose. He furrowed his brow, which was a little disconcerting given that his head was basically a skull covered in shadows.

"How long was that?" Death asked. I looked at my watch, noting the position of the hands. The time between arguments was annoyingly small.

"Two and a half hours," I said. "It's a new record!"

Death looked less than impressed by my poor enthusiasm. He looked at me, looked at Life, looked at Time, then sighed. "I am returning home," Death said. "You may stay here for a few more hours if you like, Cal, since you've been wanting a visit to the mortal realms. I trust you can find your way home."

By the time I got around to answering in the affirmative, Life was already gone and Death was fading. That left me alone with Time, who was looking mildly interested. He stood and shoved his hands into his pockets with that annoying artistic slouch again. "What's with the timer?" He asked.

I shoved my phone back into my pocket and shrugged. "For the last two weeks, every time I have had Life and Death go out together to try and sort out their differences and figure out common ground, I have timed them to see how long it would take before they started arguing. Two and half hours is actually quite the improvement for them. First time we did this, they couldn't even last through a cup of coffee."

Time chuckled. "Used to be that they were madly in love. Of course, things went wrong as they always do. Actually, that's where it all started to go badly."

"Madly in love?" I asked with a scoff. "I hardly believe it. Those two have been at each other's throats since before I got around. And then there was that whole incident with Justice—not my fault by the way. Then, Yolanda said that I had to do something about this feud before The Order of Silence got involved and forced them to spend time together in solitary confinement, which is apparently what they've done before. Apparently that didn't end well. At all. So here I am, relationship counsellor. Not in my job description, just so you know. There has to be another way." This last point was spoken mostly to myself, with my nose pinched between my fingers. Frankly, dealing with Life and Death was giving me a major headache. And no matter what I seemed to be doing, they just kept arguing. Soon, I knew there would be nothing I could do and the powers that be would have to battle it out, probably at the expense of most of the mortal realms. I hoped I was long gone by that point.

"I think there might be another way," Time said. He seemed particularly unconcerned about the situation between Life and Death. Or maybe that was just his way. Maybe he was particularly unconcerned about everything, considering that he was Time. If that was anything like what Life and Death were, then he was Time itself. Which was a terrifying thought. I narrowed my eyes a little bit.

"Oh really?" I asked. At this point, I was tired, hungry, and wanted very little more than to go and find a nice sandwich somewhere. Time nodded.

"Indeed. See, all of this started back when they were first married. They were still madly in love, only circumstances got in the way and mistakes were made. Death missed a terribly important appointment. Life refused to let Death get involved in a particular mortal's end days. Things spiralled out of control from there. But don't worry; I think you can fix it," Time said as though I was some sort of extremely powerful being of my own. I folded my arms and laughed.

"I have been trying to fix it for two weeks now, not to mention all of the minor altercations in the last year before this. Somehow, I don't think it's working." I think that might've been an understatement, but I was only human.

"I think you should give it a try my way," Time said. Before I could even ask what that meant, Time reached out and touched me on the forehead, right between my eyes.

A sharp pain formed where he touched me, like nails through my skin. The lights sharpened until they were blindingly white. The ground fell away from beneath my feet and my body felt as though it was being torn into a thousand pieces.

My last thought before I blacked out completely was that I *knew* Gilbert and Sullivan was a bad idea.

IN THE INTEREST OF TIME

I woke screaming. Now, you might think that this is a really bad way to wake up, but given my current lifestyle, it was not terribly uncommon. In fact, I had sort of lost track of the times in recent history that I had woke up with something really awful staring me in the face. Many of them, incidentally, being the selfie-loving gremlin doctor Graveltoes that was so fascinated by my humanity. Though Agravaine took particular pleasure in waking me up in unconventional ways. The incident with the tiny fire lizard? Nothing I did could possibly be considered overreaction. By contrast, staring into the face of Time was, well, pretty terrifying. Still, it was familiar.

I missed the days when waking up by means of my phone alarm was jarring.

Once my scream died down, I got a good look at the place where I was laying. Most of the time, my terrible encounters had ended with me in the hospital inElsewhere, with the weird creature Doctor Graveltoes leering over me. Well, most of the time. There was that time on the Irishman Fionn's mountain. And in a parking lot in Norway. And in the bowels of the Order of Silence's network of caves.

By contrast, the place where I was now was actually quite pleasant. It seemed like there were smoothly rolling hills, covered with waving grasses and fields. There were a few trees around and more off in the distance. Birds sang as if they hadn't a care in the world. The sun was shining. The sky was blue as it gets. On the whole, it was actually a very delightful place. But—and this was a big issue—it was not the theatre.

"Where am I?" I demanded. I tried to stand, but given that my feet seemed to have an uncertain relationship with the ground, I decided that sitting up was perhaps the best I could manage under the circumstances. Time sat on the ground beside me, his legs stretched out as if he could not be any more relaxed. Hardly a hair on his head had been ruffled. He looked around, smiling, and shrugged.

"I would've thought it obvious," he said, stretching. He stood and brushed off some of the grass from his trousers. Then, he looked around and took in a full, deep breath. Letting it out, he turned to me and smiled wider. "We're in Italy."

I coughed once. Loudly.

"Italy. Explain to me how going from a New York theatre to the Italian countryside is an obvious choice." I shoved my glasses up on my nose and shielded my eyes from the sun.

"The *where* is unimportant," Time said, shrugging dismissively. "It's the *when* that you should find interesting."

I frowned. It should have been completely and idiotically obvious given the fact that I was dealing with Time. But, call me an optimist—or an idiot—but I had hoped that maybe I wouldn't get sucked through some vortex during an average night out. "Okay, I'll bite. *When* are we?"

Time fixed me with a grin that I can only describe as mischievous elves taking too much pleasure in causing trouble. He would get along well with Agravaine and Yolanda. "I believe that you would call it the year 1494. Granted, I think you humans are very strange in the way that you describe me. The years are based on what, some arbitrary movements of the planets around the sun? Nonsense. Complete and utter nonsense."

"1494. As in the middle of the *Renaissance*. As in long before the era of indoor plumbing and the popularisation of glasses?" It had been a while since I had studied history, but I remembered a decent portion of my history lesson from Renaissance Italy, given that was when all the really good art was happening. I remembered that things had not been nearly as nice as with modern times. I remembered that the Catholic Church was in charge in a very big way. And I remembered such things like death by various unpleasant diseases, including *the plague.*

I forced my legs to cooperate and pushed myself off the ground. This time, I did manage to stand, though it was more to do with abject panic than anything else. My legs were still shaking, and I was beginning to have a splitting headache, but I managed it. Barely. I looked up at Time—still taller than me and wearing a calm expression. Time looked back and me. Smiled. That bastard.

"Indeed," he said looking around at the countryside. "Very interesting time period. Then again, they're all interesting to me."

I tried to be reasonable. I tried to think of my nice comfortable bed and my nice automatic coffeemaker. I tried to think happy thoughts, like Yolanda who efficiently sorted through my mail, electronic and otherwise, every morning before I even had to ask. I tried to think of the way that I had successfully survived my first week with Death and Life. Somehow, I imagined that the smile crossing my face wasn't quite as pleasant as I had hoped. "Would you care to tell me why we are in the middle of the Italian Renaissance? Or were you hoping I had figured that out for myself."

Time stretched lazily, looking more like he was inclined to talk nonsense than get me back to the modern times that I was used to. Sometimes, I really hated my job. "I told you," he said. "I brought you here to help. You did want to fix the problems between Life and Death, didn't you?"

This was the point where I lost my temper. I threw my arms up and practically shouted at Time. "To get them to have a normal therapy session! I didn't mean for you to go and tell me that I should be pulled through time to a place of death and disease. Take me back!"

Time seemed to consider. He looked around, put his hands in his pockets, then shook his head. "No," he said. "I don't think I will. I think this will be good for you. After all, how many people get to travel through time to help fix the wrong that was never meant to be in the first place? Appreciate the opportunities you have been given."

"I work for Death," I said through gritted teeth. "Death may have made me immortal, so I didn't fall to the ground as a dead body burnt to a crisp despite whatever stupid magic you have going on. But that doesn't mean you can just treat me like one of your playthings!"

Time paused. It was a very strange thing to see, considering every muscle in his body froze simultaneously. He just stopped. Like an actual sculpture instead of the living being that I knew he was. "No. I think this is best," Time said after a moment, his movements returning as though they had never stopped. "The other possibility is a far too… strenuous on things."

"You know that, do you?" I demanded.

Time raised an eyebrow at me. I set my jaw, but didn't rise to the bait. Yes, he was Time. Yes, he could probably see every eventuality and all of the different possibilities. But really? My life had to be involved? I had just gotten back into a good relationship with the vampires after accidentally—not my fault—killing their prince. I had gotten The Order of Silence off my back about the whole breaking the balance issue. I was just getting back into an almost normal life where I just did marketing and social media and public relations. Things were good. A decently normal life, despite my circumstances, was all I wanted. And now…

"Don't forget. An appointment. And a death meant to happen." Time raised his hand, waved, then promptly vanished. I reached out to the spot where he had been, hoping to catch a backlash or something so I could be pulled back through. Instead, I just tripped and landed on my face in the dirt. I was already hating Italy.

After a few moments, I stood up and brushed myself off. Lying in the dirt would not help the situation, as much as I wanted it to. I had to come up with a plan to get me back home, to my *normal* time of computers and plumbing and coffee. A half-formed plan took shape in the back of my mind. It was better than nothing and didn't involve Time's ridiculous errand.

If I could find Death—he was always around somewhere—then maybe I could get him to convince Time to take me back. Granted, Death would have no idea who I was given he was several centuries younger than the Death I knew, but it was worth a shot. At this point, anything would be worth a shot.

I unbuttoned my blazer, looked around to see if there were any markers to point me in the direction of civilisation, and came up with nothing. All I could see around me were fields and hills. It was very pretty.

Annoyingly pretty. This was the sort of spot I would have chosen for a nice vacation of lazy days and much wine. Only, you know, with the appropriate level of technology. This nonsense about being in 1494 was not how I had planned on a trip to Italy going. Instead of a wine tour with a nice brunette lady on my arm, I was likely to be stabbed as a heretic or a witch for wearing glasses.

"Hello there!" The voice came from behind me. I turned and tripped on a rock, falling on the ground again. There were several people on horses that I hadn't noticed before, because horses can apparently sneak up on people. They were dressed in some sort of strange clothing that reminded me of Prince Humperdinck in *The Princess Bride* movie. Tights, poofy shorts, matching tunic shirt things underneath leather armour plated with squares of metal. Two of the men had swords belted at their waist. The other carried a crossbow. They looked at me as though I were the cause of all of their problems. For all I knew, I was.

(It only occurred to me much, much later that I could not possibly be speaking English with these people. To be fair, I was severely distracted by the swords and the crossbow being pointed in my direction. I just hoped that this linguistic miracle was some byproduct of time travel and not my brain turning to mush.)

I lifted my hand and waved, trying to be friendly. I was a marketing agent. I knew how to get people to like me. Or at least buy into whatever I was selling, which was pretty much the same thing. "Hello there," I said, smiling and realising too late that I had perfect teeth in a time when dentistry was probably mostly pulling teeth out. "I seem to be lost."

"Oh, indeed you are," the man with the crossbow said. "You are not from around here, are you? I would suggest you get off the land of my very wealthy employers and go find somewhere else to peddle your wares."

"Peddle my what?"

The man on the left gestured with his sword to my clothing. It occurred to me that I was wearing things that didn't look exactly like they belonged in the late 15th century of Italy. In fact, given the glasses, my modern hair, my teeth, and the fact that I wasn't malnourished or short, I figured I probably looked like a madman.

"I think there has been some sort of misunderstanding," I said, holding my hands up. It didn't even occur to me that people might not care what I was saying. I just talked and gave my best smile to make them feel non-threatened. Given that I was a fairly nonthreatening person, I figured that would go pretty well. Until they pointed weapons at me.

"I suggest you leave now, before we decide that being paid to defend Florence includes chasing off the likes of you," the middle man spoke again. I nodded, considered my options, and took the most obvious course: I started running.

Now, as out of place as my modern and very stylish clothing was in this Italian countryside of a different time, I can tell you that my shoes were really, really out of place.

Some things you shouldn't run in, and patent leather Italian loafers—yes, I note the irony of wearing Italian loafers in Renaissance Italy—are one such example. I was soon tripping and trying very hard not to fall on my face, again, when I heard the unmistakable laughter and beat of horses hooves behind. They were running me down.

If you find yourself in similar circumstances as these, I can give you some advice: sheer desperation counts for a lot. I put on a burst of speed and managed to fall into a hidden gully surrounded by trees and bushes that had definitely not been there a few seconds before. Water surged past my ankles and I slipped, getting mud everywhere. I heard that laughter again behind me and glanced over my shoulder. The three men were pointing at me and laughing as if I was the funniest thing they'd seen in their lifetime. I decided I wasn't going to wait around to find out if they wanted to follow up on their part of this ridiculous charade, pulled myself to my feet and ran along the creek bed. My shoes squelched unpleasantly.

"Over here," a voice called from the other side of the low gully. Looking through the trees, I saw another man, dressed very similarly to the others minus the armour, which made him look far less threatening. I was all for less-threatening. He was maybe twenty-five, twenty-seven or so. He was wearing a long tunic, some sort of weird robe thing that went to the knees, a belt around his waist, stockings and soft leather shoes. His hair went to his chin and he had some sort of velvet cap. The colours were relatively wild, considering that the men on the horses had worn subdued leather and greys or browns. This man wore black with bright green trim and even yellow on his tunic. *When in Rome,* I thought.

I was definitely not in Rome, by the way. I think.

I clambered out of the gully to stand next to the man, breathing heavily and resting my hands on my knees as I did so. When I got the job with Death, circumstances had forced me to get more in shape, but there are very few things that prepare you for running and tripping through the hills while being chased by horses and men with weapons, then falling into a creek at the bottom of a shallow gully. It was just that sort of day.

"I think you should come with me," the mysterious man said. "They should leave you alone once you're in the city. And they wouldn't dare hurt me."

"Are you sure about that?" I asked, wincing as my voice squeaked at the end of my question. I cleared my throat and straightened, trying to look as intimidating as possible. Not the easiest thing to do when your clothes are covered in mud and your bowtie is coming undone. "I have a feeling they're not the sort to give up easily."

"Mercenaries aren't, usually. But they have far better things to do than run after a scrawny foreigner like you. It's market day and they have to oversee the merchants coming in and out, checking for the French."

"I have no idea what you're talking about, but as long as I'm not dead and you can get me to the city, I thank you very much," I said, holding out my hand. My new friend looked at it, looked at me, looked at my hand again. I lowered my hand and cursed silently. When was the handshake invented?

"You are very strange," the man said. "Where are you from?"

"A place very far away from here. You wouldn't have heard of it."

Though, to be fair, England was very much around in the fifteenth century. I decided it was better to just lie, in case anyone decided to ask me questions about my jolly homeland.

"I have learned all of the peoples and places in the known world," the man said proudly. I doubted that was the case, considering that America had only been discovered by Columbus a couple of years before. But weren't the Dutch there first? And then there was Antartica, and Australia. I wished desperately for Google just then.

"I'm from…Norway," I said, thinking of the first name that popped into my mind. Actually, I had briefly been in Norway the year before and found it a very pleasant place. Compared to Renaissance Italy, that is.

"Norway? Do you mean Scandinavia?"

I shrugged and tried to wipe some of the mud off my clothes. "Yep. Scandinavia."

"See? I am familiar with the place. Now, follow me. Florence is this way." The man started walking. He then paused and turned back to me. "By the way, my name is Machiavelli. Niccolo Machiavelli."

I gave a high, very uncertain laugh. "Cal Thorpe," I said. Because my day couldn't really get any worse.

The first opportunity, I was going to give Time a piece of my very, very unhappy mind. And then I was going to take a vacation.

TIME MARCHES ON

I followed Machiavelli through the countryside towards what looked to be a walled city built by the finest hands history had seen. The buildings that were visible over the wall were both grand and terrible. Some were larger than life. Others were comparatively shoddy craftsmanship—but still better than any modern concrete building—from an earlier or poorer time. Machiavelli had told me that this was Florence. Some vague history lesson told me that this was the height of the Renaissance and possibly also the centre of it, too, but given my propensity for inaccurate guesses it was quite possible that things were not as I thought they were. I really hoped they were. If there was one thing I was going to get out of this whole situation, it was that DaVinci was alive at this point.

"You perhaps shouldn't have gotten involved with them," Machiavelli said as we approached the city. He looked back at me, casual as can be, as though he weren't some horrid politician person who basically invented the cutthroat ideas behind the modern world. Though, he seemed a little young to have been a political mastermind. "They are not the nicest bunch."

"You know, I figured that out," I said. "It might have something to do with the fact that they tried to shoot at me with their crossbows. Or dismember me. That could have been it, too."

"That would be because you messed up their hunt," Machiavelli said. "They're rather an entitled bunch, those mercenaries. Necessary, but entitled. And you are rather stupid for getting in their way."

"I didn't intentionally get in their way," I grumbled. I tripped over some loose gravel in the road and had to remind myself that I was in the fifteenth century before I started complaining about road repair. I mean, for goodness sakes, Machiavelli was escorting me. *The* Machiavelli. Not to mention I had stowed my glasses in my pocket, I was fairly certain that shoe laces hadn't been invented yet and who knows what they would do with me if they found my phone, even powered down. Then, the city of Florence rose above me and I had to pause for a moment to take in what I was seeing.

I had been all over the magical realms of Elsewhere. I had seen Death's manse, Life's castle, the overly-extravagant and poorly decorated home of the vampires. I had seen magical beings that were larger than life and twice as beautiful (also, deadly, but still). What I hadn't been prepared for was walking into the heart of Italy at the height of the Renaissance.

From the outside, Florence looked like a walled city

made with stone. It was interesting, and the stones fit together quite well, but it was just a city. As we passed through the gates, things changed. I saw buildings that were shown on modern postcards that were still in prime condition. Stonework that was carved intricately and masterfully. Statues graced courtyards and public squares held fountains that were stunningly beautiful. The streets were cobbled, though still dirty. People walked about wearing clothes that looked to me like they came straight from paintings by DaVinci or Michaelangelo. Trade was bustling. People handed goods—things that we rarely ever saw in these qualities in the future—back in exchange for money. People talked and laughed and children ran around. People sat in the squares and exchanged news. It was a bustling city. One of life and art and wealth.

And here I was, being led by a figure known for his dangerous political thinking.

Great. Just great.

"I would say that intent had little to do with your situation," Machiavelli said. He waved to a few people whenever we passed public squares. I didn't know where we were going, but we obviously had a destination. Part of me wanted to explore. Then, I caught whiff of some of the people we passed and decided that I would much rather have modern conveniences like daily showers than explore fifteenth century Italy. "There are some who would happily hunt you down, simply because you are different than they. Especially now, with everyone on edge."

"…On edge?" I asked. In my experience, on edge

meant that my boss or his wife were somewhere nearby. Could it really be that easy? Could I find Life and Death and solve all my problems in less than a day? I mentally cursed myself for even thinking it. Things were never that easy.

Machiavelli turned and stared at me. "Do you not know? The invasion? King Charles VIII, of France, has foolishly decided that we are to be his next conquests. And there has been a resurgence of plague, though that is to be expected. It is the French that are more concerning."

I looked around, half expecting to be arrested or killed by French soldiers just as soon as we turned the next corners. It would be just my luck to have survived facing down all sorts of nasties to be killed by humans in a time before the French press. There would be some sort of dramatic irony about the situation. Death would probably approve. Machiavelli just snorted and clapped me on the shoulder.

"There is no need to fear. You will not be caught by soldiers," he said. "Florence has not yet been reached by the French. And, with some strategy and action, they may never reach here at all. *That* is why the mercenaries are here, despite their proclivities towards harassing people to assuage their boredom."

I wished desperately for access to the Internet just then. Or, at the very least, a history book. Instead, I shoved my hands in my pockets and held onto my phone tightly. It, and my glasses, were the few reminders I had that this wasn't a dream. Machiavelli looked at me with his head tilted.

"You are strange, to have not heard of such current events," he said. "What far corners of the world have you been in Cal Thorpe, to be so out of touch? Surely you could not have come all the way from Scandinavia and still be so ignorant of the region's machinations."

I winced and looked around the square where we had finally stopped walking. "Oh, you know, here and there. Nowhere nearby. It's...I have been out of touch for a while."

Machiavelli nodded solemnly. "Yes. I can see that." Then, he grinned and grabbed my arm, turning me towards one of the stone buildings. I heard laughter coming from within and there was a scent that wasn't entirely unpleasant. "Come! We'll get you a drink and something to eat and then you can tell me your tale!"

"Oh, ah, that's very kind but..." I started, then trailed off. I had spotted something across the square from the little pub that was awfully familiar. Actually, it was a he and he was familiar because I was responsible for his death. Or, I would be in about five hundred years or so. Thaddeus, the vampire prince who had tried to drink my blood while I was unkillable—Death's fault, not mine—and ended up poofed as a result. It had granted me permanent enmity from the vampire race, despite the fact that they desperately wanted me to work for them because I was in marketing.

It's a long story.

Despite my blurry vision, I would have bet money on the figure being the vampire prince. Thaddeus was dressed as poorly, and as grandly, as I remembered. He wore some sort of long tunic in a deep fascia with blue sleeves, over hose of a garish green. Somehow, the colours did manage to work together, except for the fact that they clashed with his extraordinarily pale skin. He was being followed around by a servant—a hobgoblin, I believe—who carried a flat sort of parasol to keep off the sun. Thaddeus did not look happy and I did not want to get in his way. Besides, whatever a vampire prince was doing in Florence, I doubted it would be good.

I was a little surprised that people weren't screaming and freaking out, considering a vampire and hobgoblin were walking through the square without a guise. At least, not one that I could see, though that didn't mean a lot. I couldn't see many things without my glasses. Who was to say a guise would be any different. Somehow, I doubted that it was my eyes that were the problem.

"Ah, them," Machiavelli said with a casual shrug, noticing my staring. "I would not worry overmuch about the Medici. They are more benevolent than their reputations would suggest."

"The *who*?!" I asked, my voice squeaking. This was one history lesson I didn't actually need a refresher on. I knew full well who the Medici were. Like Machiavelli, they had survived the ravages of time and their names were remembered far too well in the future. They were the uber-powerful merchant family who basically ruled Florence, if not all of Italy, during the Renaissance. Them and the supremely dangerous

Borgias. Basically, they were In Charge. And now I understood that they were vampires, too.

Actually, that explained a lot about history.

Machiavelli turned again towards the pub tavern thing and pushed on, ignoring Thaddeus completely. I decided upon the lesser of two evils and followed. Inside, the building was pretty much what I had come to expect from a pub in the Elsewhere. It was low-ceilinged, there were tables surrounded by people, a fireplace sat roaring in the corner—both for cooking and warmth, even on this spring day—and the noise was an uncomfortable level of yelling to be heard. Only, instead of being habited by denizens of Elsewhere, this one was populated by mostly human people. I say mostly, because there were a few glints of not-quite-human features here and there. I had a feeling that the supernatural creatures were wearing guises, which confirmed my theory about the vampiric Medici being too powerful to bother with. That, or Italy was a far more interesting place than I thought.

"Wine!" Machiavelli called. He strode across the room to sit with a few other people of about his age, wearing clothes of similar style and garish colouring. He was greeted boisterously and I was somehow pulled into the festivities. Names were passed around, but I didn't recognise a single one and as a result, they flew in one ear and out the other. I tried to hold onto the names, but I had a hard enough time in my own time, not to mention with a bunch of dead guys.

"Cal Thorpe here is from Scandinavia. He has been travelling and does not seem to know what is going on in the world," Machiavelli said as a summation of my story once the others' names had been passed around. "I found him being chased by some Medici mercenaries intent on spearing him for their hunt."

"Does not know what is going on in the world?" a man asked, short and with a wide, frog-mouthed grin. "I spent a holiday like that once. The woman was very pleased with me when I was done!"

I chuckled awkwardly, trying to remind myself why I was here. Everyone else laughed raucously and passed around another jug of wine. I really wanted some water, but after taking a sip of the wine, I decided it would suffice. Actually, it would more than suffice. It was exquisite.

I like to think of myself as a fairly decent wine connoisseur. In my years of marketing, I had wined and dined with a fair number of clients. It had gotten to the point where I could tell a good bottle from a bad. And I generally enjoyed the good. But sitting in that little late fifteenth century tavern, for lack of a better word, drinking fine Italian wine, that was an entirely different experience. I could tell that the wine was a little sour, perhaps not aged near as nicely as it could've been. And, by Florence standards, it was likely average. But to me, it just exploded in my mouth. I was suddenly looking a little bit more kindly towards Time for disposing of me in the fifteenth century. Perhaps this assignment wouldn't be quite so dismal after all.

"You're a strange one," one of Machiavelli's friends said. He watched me take another sip of the wine, savouring the flavours. I shrugged.

"That he is," Machiavelli agreed, grinning at me. He sat up straighter and looked at me with some sort of odd pride, as though he had found an unusually ugly stray dog that he intended to tame. "Completely politically ignorant. He nearly panicked at the site of one of the Medici walking across the square."

"The Medici They may be rich, they may be powerful, but there in nothing compared to the dangers that we face these days. That absurd King Charles, for instance, is a far more potent threat."

"What will happen when he gets here? Will you just fight him?" I asked, taking another large mouthful of wine. The people around the table looked at me as though I were insane. In some instances, they might have been right. Today I was just ignorant. Well... mostly. I was feeling a little insane, but felt it perfectly justified given the situation in which I found myself.

Machiavelli looked at me with a worried frown, his brows drawn together. "We have no standing army, no soldiers. If Charles gets this far, we will have to pull together every scrap of income that we have in order to pay for an army. Those mercenaries outside are already perhaps more than can be afforded and the Signori do not wish to pay for more, which is why they are loyal to the Medici name and purse."

An army of angry, underpaid mercenaries like the ones that had chased me earlier were all that was standing between Florence and the distant French. Great. I hoped I wouldn't be here that long. I was about to turn the direction of the conversation in a different direction—preferably one wherein we ordered more wine—when two figures stepped through the door of the pub. I swore I recognised one almost immediately, which was near about impossible as she was meant to be in the twenty-first century, organising my paperwork.

I leapt up and ran towards her, joy overriding my sense of caution. I was that relieved she was here. "Yolanda!" I stopped a few inches from polite distance away, looking at the woman with a grin that was likely doing me no favours. She was tall, stocky, possessed of more muscles than many bodybuilders I had known, with straight brown hair, and a massive sword across her back, which would be completely out of time even for what I knew of the fifteenth century. I had figured she was my assistant, wearing a guise as she usually did when coming to the mortal realms. Instead, I got a good glare the likes of which I had not felt in quite some time. Not even from The Order of Silence, who hated me unambiguously.

"I beg your pardon?" she asked, enunciating each word so I could be sure of her full displeasure. I saw her reach for a dagger at her waist. Desperately, I looked to her shorter companion for help, or perhaps a more accurate identification. My eyes were as wide as they could go, but I was still blind. I peered closer and realised, too late, my mistake.

The smaller woman—and by smaller, I mean only very slightly shorter than myself—was wearing a dress typical of the time, though a bit shorter in the ankle so the movement was swift and easy. She had darker hair than her companion, tied up in some sort of elaborate braid thing. At her waist was a pouch with some feathers sticking out of it, and a roll of papers. She folded her arms in a thoroughly modern gesture and looked me up and down, raising her eyebrows. "I don't know what a Yolanda is, but her name is Charlotte."

"Charlotte the Unkillable," the very dangerous woman added with a ferocious grin.

"So…not Yolanda. Not a rock troll." As soon as the words left my mouth, I knew they were the absolute wrong thing to say. First off, I had to be aware that I was once again dealing with mortals. People who had no idea of the supernatural and the magical, even considering the fact that they had vampires walking among them as their ruling family. Granted, these two seemed to be unusual for the time—even taking my limited experience into account—but the point still stood.

At my words, these two reacted in a spectacular fashion. The smaller one straightened, eyes unbelievably wide and arms stiff at her sides. Charlotte the Unkillable drew the massive sword and pointed it at my neck. The rest of the pub had gone completely silent. I flicked my eyes over my shoulder and saw Machiavelli staring at me as though I was about to die. This time, I didn't have Death on hand to help me.

"I think maybe this isn't what you think it is," I said. I raised my hands up, showing that I had no weapons. "My name is Cal Thorpe. I thought you were somebody else. You have my sincerest apologies, and I hope you have a super fantastic day."

Charlotte took in a deep breath, looked around at

the comparatively puny humans in the pub—all of whom were staring at us—and put her sword away. A collective sigh of relief was released, and conversation started up again, though not nearly at the level that it had been before. More than one person moved as far away from us as they could.

"I am not a rock troll," Charlotte said, leaning in close to whisper the words in my ear. At this point, I had the feeling my eyes were as wide as dinner saucers. They knew what I was talking about. Maybe they could help me find Life and Death. On the other hand, they could have thought I was crazy. That seemed far more likely.

The shorter woman leaned in close also. "She's a giantess. We've been out adventuring, so it's possible that's why you haven't heard of us."

They didn't think I was crazy! Well, completely crazy.

"I've been out of touch," I said. "And you are?"

"I have no name. I am simply The Author," the woman said with a sniff. She looked around in some sort of mysterious fashion, but by eye roll Charlotte presented, I got the impression that this was more a hopeful descriptor than an actual one.

I nodded and was about to ask more questions, like what a giantess was doing in the mortal realms and could I beg her help, when someone tapped me on my shoulder. I jumped and let out a squeak. Machiavelli looked at me as though I were slightly crazy. This was becoming a common look.

"Is everything well here?" he asked.

"I thought I recognised her," I said with a smile most commonly reserved for the president of my former marketing company. "I was mistaken. No hard feelings."

"Hard...feelings? I am not familiar with that phrase," Machiavelli said. I just nodded and smiled and shrugged. Perhaps I should been asking why it was that he could understand me in the first place, but I decided not to ponder on things that would probably break my brain.

"Where can I find a place to stay?" I asked instead of explaining myself. "I don't really have any money and I don't really know where to go to earn money around here. And I don't know where to find the people I'm looking for."

Yes, Cal, when in doubt of being considered insane, just change the subject. That won't confuse anybody.

"I have a spare room," Machiavelli said with a frown. "I would worry about your character, but so far I have seen nothing at fault except a general inclination toward stupidity. I believe that can be remedied."

I smiled and gave an awkward chuckle. "Thanks so much," I said dryly. "But still does not help my issue regarding funding."

"The city watch will hire you on a temporary basis," Machiavelli said. He eyed the enormous sword strapped to Charlotte's back. "They take on just about anybody, as long as you can stay awake through the night. Not permanently, perhaps, but long enough for you to earn money. Or you can get work with some of the farmers outside the city. Perhaps doing building works, as there are many buildings and systems being improved. But...I would suggest the city guard. They are perhaps the least discerning."

"Absolutely," I said, ignoring the insult. If only these people knew where I was from and what sort of technology I had access to and what sort of things I had done. I mean, I had stood up to an immortal Irishman, a vampire horde, an extremely angry detective, the embodiment of Justice, and managed to create a viable public relations and marketing firm for the supernatural and magically inclined. Instead, these people all watched me, expecting me to perform another extremely stupid act.

"Very good," Machiavelli said. He gestured toward the door. "We will go talk to them now. Before you get yourself into further trouble, perhaps."

I nodded and followed him. Charlotte called out, making me turn back and look at her.

"I have questions for you, Cal Thorpe," she said pointing an accusing finger in my direction. "I will be finding you later this evening. And you had better have answers for me."

With that, I left Charlotte the Unkillable and The Author behind, half of me relieved, the other half worried. Maybe I should have shrugged Machiavelli off and remained behind to talk with them. They were perhaps my best chance of getting out of this miserable —if artistically inclined—pit. But something told me that I hadn't run into Machiavelli by chance. Time could have easily dropped me off at any point; instead, he chose the one instance where it would be almost impossible not to run into Machiavelli. Given that he was, well, Time, I was inclined to believe that this was important.

That didn't mean I *liked* it, but it was probably important.

I would just have to wait for Charlotte to find me and hope that she was willing to help me after I accidentally insulted her.

I followed Machiavelli through the streets of Florence to a building attached to the wall. I'm afraid I rather gawked on the way, but most people just took this as the idiot foreigner—apparent by the out-of-place clothes I was wearing—being stupidly impressed with their city. Frankly, they were right. Their city was stupidly impressive.

Not an hour later, I found myself decked out in a leather jacket-like-armour-thing that was extremely uncomfortable and smelled of sweat. At least it wasn't metal plate armour, as I saw a couple of people wearing. The city watch commander seemed inclined to believe Machiavelli when he explained about me. I hadn't even had to answer any questions, like was I actually able to wield a weapon. (Hint: the answer was no.) They put me on duty at one of the small gates in the wall that led to a lesser used path, which was perfectly fine with me. I was holding a pike which was really tall, and standing at one of the gates making sure that no one came in without a good reason. I could wallow in misery in peace. Honestly, as far as first days go, I was beyond the point of wishing for a computer and a drink that wasn't wine.

Frankly, I wasn't very good at the whole city watch

thing. I had been informed by a surly old man with a long beard that I was meant to be keeping watch over this tiny little gate, and that if anyone wanted to get through, I was to question them until they decided better of it and would come back in the morning. After about five hours of standing around in the dark, I had encountered one dog, a flock of chickens being led by a tiny girl who looked at me with such pleading in her eyes that I immediately stepped aside without any questions, and a goat. The goat had tried to eat my leather-jacket-armour-thing. I had tried to push it back with my pike and ended up simply making it mad instead. It stared at me with those strange slitted eyes. Which is how I found myself having a staring contest with a goat when Charlotte the Unkillable appeared out of the shadows like magic.

"You are strange," she said. I yelped and leapt backwards, hitting my head on the gate itself. Charlotte stood there with her hands on her hips, legs spread wide and what appeared to be a fighting stance. Her small companion, The Author, just chuckled.

"Do you enjoy sneaking up on people?" I asked, rubbing the back of my head. Charlotte shrugged and nodded.

"What I want to know," she said, taking a seat on a conveniently placed stone and next to the gate, "is why a time walker is here."

I blinked. "A time walker?"

"A time walker is a being who walks through time, using the Elsewhere as a means of transportation due to its ambient magic. It can be sometimes unpredictable, but it is often a fast and easy way to step through time in order to experience the interesting and pertinent parts of history," The Author said. I nodded as solemnly as I could after her long-winded explanation. Oddly enough, I understood most of what she was saying. Yolanda had schooled me on the ambient magics of Elsewhere, warning me to be extremely careful when performing rituals. I had responded with the fact that I was human, ignorant, and had no idea what she was talking about and was therefore unlikely to be able to be careful when performing magic at all, let alone a ritual that I probably wouldn't ever use.

"Ignore her," Charlotte said. She waved her hand dismissively at The Author, who took a seat at the base of the rock and pulled out her scroll and feather, tied to a piece of charcoal. She started scribbling. "She follows me around because she finds it entertaining to transcribe my stories. I accidentally picked her up in the 1600s, stranded there on an unfortunate journey from your world war. I don't remember which one. She called herself a journalist. But, no one knows what a journalist is."

"I know what a journalist is," I said. Charlotte raised an eyebrow. She looked around, spotting the goat sneaking up on her. She fixed it with a singular glare and it scampered off. "Ah, you mean from the time periods in which you are accustomed to working. I thought your sword didn't quite fit fifteenth century Italy. Not to mention the fact that you're wearing men's clothes."

"See? A time walker," Charlotte said. She rested an

elbow on a knee and leaned in closer, staring at me. I did my best not to fidget. "The question is, once again, what a time walker is doing here. And a particularly incompetent one at that."

"I could ask the same of you," I said with as much snark as I could muster. "What is a giantess —"

"Half giantess," Charlotte corrected, glaring at The Author who was still scribbling away.

"Okay. What is a half giantess doing here? These people seem extraordinarily ordinary except for the vampires that are running loose."

"This place is an interesting confluence of people. They have an unusual collection of magical artefacts, which I happen to be trying to find. Wait…did you say vampires?" Charlotte raised her eyebrows at me again. I shrugged and tugged at the neck of the stupid leather armour thing that was doing its best to choke me.

"I recognised one from across the square. We had dealings before. Or rather, will have dealings in the future. I hate time travel. None of the verbs make sense. Anyways, Machiavelli claims that this vampire is one of the Medici. From what I understand that is one of the people in charge, which I definitely don't remember from my history lessons. I want to know why vampires are running Florence." I pinched the bridge of my nose. "Actually no. I'm here for an entirely different reason. That just struck me as quite unusual."

"And what is the reason that brought you here?" Charlotte asked, folding her arms.

I waffled for a moment, shifting my weight back and forth and debating how much to tell her. I mean, I didn't really trust her. We had only just met. And as far as I could tell, she was a treasure hunter looking for an adventure. Not to mention a time walker unfamiliar with the local culture, which apparently I was, too. Though not by choice. Then again, I was pretty much on my own in the fifteenth century, except for a strangely-benevolent Machiavelli who would later be known for his political scheming. Not to mention, I needed to find Life and Death rather sooner than later. I would have to maybe trust Charlotte.

"How connected are you to the magical community?" I asked instead. Charlotte took in a deep breath through the nose and adjusted the sword across her back so that it sat more comfortably.

"Fairly connected. I have been in this time for a while, but I know my way around. I could find you the underground community in Florence, if that is what you're looking for. But you haven't answered my question," she said looking at me with a cunning grin. It was a little incongruence on her face, given that she looked more like she would happily play the Hulk in any television show. But I got the impression that Charlotte the Unkillable was more than she appeared. I wasn't quite so sure about The Author though.

"Okay. Here's what I propose. I'll help you find your magical artefacts if you help me," I said. The Author looked up.

"But who are you? What's your story? How do you fit into the larger plot?" She asked, pointing her charcoal at me. I exchanged a glance with Charlotte who shook her head and rolled her eyes. I pushed my finger up the bridge of my nose, feeling a little lost when my glasses weren't there, then shook my head. I couldn't really see anything else for it but to just tell these two everything. After all, they had only threatened me once and that was mostly my fault. For once.

"Journalist. Right. Okay, well I guess I will start from the beginning. I'm Cal Thorpe, I work for Death as his public relations manager. I was out with Death and Life, dealing with some relationship issues between the two, when Time stepped in and sent me here to fix things." I spread my hands in a tada gesture which I accompanied with a winning smile. The goat bleated, but that was the only reaction I got. Charlotte stared at me with her mouth open. The author was fish eyed and dropped her charcoal on the ground.

Charlotte turned to The Author and pointed an angry finger at her. "This is your fault. You're the one who said that it would be interesting to see Italy."

"Isn't this interesting? We've never met anyone who works for Death before. You're the adventurer. I'm pretty sure this counts as an adventure." The Author picked up her charcoal and started scribbling furiously again. Charlotte flexed her fingers in and out of a fist, like she would very much like to hit her companion. She visibly took in a breath, counted, then let it out slowly. Finally, Charlotte folded her hands together and set them neatly in her lap.

"She has...a point. Unfortunately. That is rather the point of an adventure. Adapt to the times. All right, Cal Thorpe. You have yourself a deal. We'll help you 'fix things' and you help us find the artefact." Charlotte held out her hand. I hesitated for half a second before I shook it. My hesitation had little to do with distrusting Charlotte the Unkillable, and more to do with the fact that I was having one of those very strange days.

"It would be my pleasure," I said. I fidgeted for a moment, looking at the overly large blade on Charlotte's back and watching the author scribble. "Why do they call you Unkillable? I mean, I was unkillable once, but that was more of an accident than anything."

Charlotte sighed and shook her head. "I think some things are better left unsaid. Why don't you tell me more about working for Death?"

"Actually, I'm more interested in how it is that I came to meet Machiavelli and a time walking half giantess with her journalist companion in the same day," I said. "This is one of those things that has me thinking Life got involved. She's tricky like that... Maybe it will be easier than I thought to figure out what she wants from me."

TIME OF DEATH

At the end of my watch—for which I felt extraordinarily unqualified, but considering the worst thing I had to fend off was a goat, I was still pleased—I managed to follow the precise instructions Machiavelli gave me for how to get back to his house. I was stumbling along the darkened cobbled streets and wishing for Google Maps. I felt the familiar weight of my phone against my leg and took a deep breath. It would be of no help to me. My familiar comfort was nothing more than a weight in my pocket. Then, glancing at the street, I found I recognised it. Not only that, but Machiavelli was standing in the doorway, waiting for me with an amused smile.

My shoulders straightened at that tiny victory. It was silly, really. I'd not only had Machiavelli go over the directions with me three times, but he walked me from the house to the guardhouse. After receiving my measly pay for a night's work, I had managed to make it back to my destination without any help. Money in my pocket and that tiny victory had me feeling like I could take on a particularly irked hobgoblin.

The result was that I was fairly sauntering up to Machiavelli as dawn hit. He looked at me with a smirk. "I take it things did not go too badly?" He asked.

I shrugged. "I think I might have accidentally let in a girl and some chickens, but otherwise it was fairly quiet. I'm surprised that your city is so free with their guard positions."

Machiavelli turned and gestured me inside. The little house was connected to the buildings next to it and I expected it to be much like the pub from the day before. But this was cosier and somehow more comforting, as well as amazingly extravagant and exactly what I would expect from the height of the Renaissance. The floor was stone except for where a few small handwoven rugs had been laid down. A cat lay on those, claws happily tearing apart good crafts-manship. A wooden table with vines carved up the legs sat in the far corner of the room, next to a fire with an iron grate, probably for cooking of some sort. There were several dead birds, all plucked, sitting on the table. A small wooden icon hung on the wall next to the stairs. In all, it was far more comfortable than I had anticipated. Except for the lack of running water, the lack of modern cooking supplies, it felt much like my own home.

"We have had some difficult times recently," Machi-avelli explained after a moment, apparently consid-ering my question to be a serious press for information. He didn't bother to elaborate further. I had a feeling that the French were not the only problems facing this city.

He led me up the stairs to a room with a small bed, also intricately carved but somehow still simple. "This is for you."

With that declaration, he sighed and shook his head, leaning against the doorframe. "There have been political machinations that have made Florence perhaps more vulnerable than otherwise. The Medici are struggling against Savonarola, who has been off causing them a few problems. That unrest trickles down to the rest of us comparatively lowly sorts. So, the city guard must get its people where it can."

"You're going to have problems if they keep it up," I pointed out. Machiavelli nodded, giving me a mischievous grin.

"It will not be boring, that is certain," he said. "Now, get some sleep. I have things to attend to and you look as though you will collapse at any moment."

I nodded and before I could formulate a properly grateful response, Machiavelli was gone and I was asleep on an extraordinarily uncomfortable bed. It didn't occur to me until I woke up some seven hours later, that I had been awake for approximately forty-eight hours. Going out with Life and Death, being transported to Italy, where I was chased, became probably drunk, then sat up all night guarding a city that wasn't even my own with a half-giantess…it had been a rather busy couple of days.

I woke with sunlight streaming through my eyes. My mouth tasted like old carpet and I realised, only after instinctively moving to put my glasses on, that I was not in a place where that would be a good idea. I sat up and looked around, hoping to find a washbasin or something. I had a feeling a toothbrush would be way, way out of the question. Actually, I didn't have any idea what people did for their teeth in 1494, but given the teeth I had seen thus far, I had a feeling it had little to do with toothpaste and floss. I did spot a basin and pitcher, which was half-full of water. I poured it out over my head, shocking me into alertness, then used what little remained to swish around my mouth and prayed for the best. Hopefully I wouldn't be here long enough to require what these people used for a dentist.

Then, I spotted something sitting on a stool by the door. It was a pile of fabric. Actually, it was several different fabrics. I went through the pile and found a whole collection of fairly interesting pieces of clothing that I assumed I was meant to wear. By the time I figured out what went where, I was sure I looked like a fool. Compared to the clothing Machiavelli was wearing yesterday, this felt…uncomfortably risqué. I had a tunic doublet thing which dipped quite low on the chest, revealing the shirt beneath. The tunic doublet thing that the other men I had seen wearing went almost to their knees. Mine did not. It hit about mid thigh and left the rest of my legs—thankfully covered in a strange pair of beige-yellow tights or leggings or something. The worst part was a codpiece, which presence was enough to make me want to beat Time quite thoroughly.

I tugged the doublet as far down as it would go in a

desperate attempt to retain my dignity while trying to tug my boots higher. I felt like I was in a Shakespearean play, prancing about for everyone to see. Not particularly masculine, let me tell you. The leather jacket armour thing had been far better than this, even with the old sweat smell.

After a few moments of trying to make the clothes better, the door opened and Machiavelli peered in. He saw me awake, standing, looking like a fool, and nodded. "Good. You look normal, now. You must have been out of touch for a very long time to wear such obviously foreign clothing. No one will trust you unless you can act like you have at least tried to adopt our customs."

I gave a weak laugh and resisted the urge to try and reposition the codpiece. "Yeah. Scandinavia. We, ah, get colder weather there than here. It's…different."

All I received for that response was a raised eyebrow. My host shook his head then retreated, obviously intending me to follow. I did. Downstairs had changed in the few hours that I had slept. Now there were papers and things strewn about the table instead of the dead birds. I saw something that looked suspiciously like verse, which Machiavelli swept up quickly, eyes fixed on the table. Interesting.

He sat and pushed a plate of bread with some cheese in my direction. "So!" he said, perhaps too brightly. "What is it that brings you to Florence? We had little time to talk yesterday, with all of the events that seemed to befall you. Are you here to perhaps trade? Or are you a French spy?"

I spluttered at that last one, nearly choking on the bread. Machiavelli poured me a glass of watered-down wine and I drank it eagerly before I realised what it was. That made me cough all the harder. Eventually, I managed to get my lungs under control. I looked up and glared at Machiavelli, who was doing a poor job of trying to conceal his laughter. At my look, he burst out into full belly laughs.

"Your face! Oh, what a sight!" he said, pointing at me. I sighed.

"Why would you do that to me?" I asked, sniffing. Machiavelli shook his head, still lost in the throes of laughter. "I'm not a French spy."

"I did not believe you were," he said, wiping tears from his eyes. "You dress like a foreigner, get lost at the drop of a hat, and your idioms are unusual. No French spy would be so careless in their execution. Not to mention, you nearly got your head taken off by that woman yesterday. A woman!"

I frowned and tore off more of my bread. Right. This was before the whole feminist movement. Way, *way* before. "Women can be quite dangerous," I said, wondering if it would be possible to instil a sense of decency into the past.

Machiavelli nodded. "Indeed, sir! I have met many women whose minds are as subtle as snakes. But never before have I seen one wield a greatsword of that size. She looked quite formidable."

I settled for the half victory and finished off my food. "You wouldn't happen to know where, ah, Lorenzo de Medici lives? I'm meeting that woman—

Charlotte—there later. She has some business and wants my help."

I think I managed to stun my host for the first time since meeting him. Machiavelli's eyes bugged out and his mouth gaped open and shut like a mute parrot. After a moment, he closed his mouth and just stared at me. I waited.

"You obviously have a death wish."

Well, yes, I was asking to be led into a den of vampires, but I didn't think that Machiavelli *knew* that. Besides, it wasn't like I hadn't dealt with vampires before, in the future. A few well-placed compliments, a few suggestions on how to improve their image recognition and poof, they practically fell at my feet. After trying to kill me. Still. This time, though, I would have Charlotte the Unkillable and her strange companion to help. It might not be rock troll battle magic, like my assistant Yolanda had, but I had a feeling it would do in a pinch.

"What makes you say that?" I asked. "I thought you said the Medici were more benevolent than their reputation suggested."

"You misunderstand. The Medici fairly run Florence. They are bankers and merchants in a city built on trade. If you come across them in the street, they are not likely to do you any harm; they may even buy from merchants and tradespeople. Dealing with them personally, however...They do not have the full authority of the Church behind them, not with Savanarola, but they certainly have enough power to stand up to the aspects of the Church they dislike. Anyone who can do that and still live—and live well—is a force to fear. I may be from a land-owning family, but I am poor and have no real presence as anything more than a scribe. I would not be able to see them if I scraped my forehead on the stones at their door. You, a foreigner, with no real product to trade, would not be allowed near. Not with all the unrest that Savanarola has been raising. My advice is: if the Medici are your business here in Florence, find another business."

All this and they were vampires. Yeah, maybe not my best idea. Still, I had little choice unless I wanted to walk away from Charlotte's assistance and instead slit my own wrists to try and gain Death's attention. I doubted that would work very well.

"Unfortunately, the matter is fixed," I said. "I have, ah, reasonable confidence that things will go well. Ish. All I need is a point in the right direction. Please."

Machiavelli ran his hand through his chin-length hair. He looked around his house, then looked over at me. After a few moments, he frowned and pointed at me accusingly. "Very well. I shall help you. But I warn you now: this will end poorly. One way or another, this will end very poorly."

I nodded and fixed a falsely-bright smile on my face in the hopes of being encouraging. "I am extremely familiar with the concept."

Machiavelli responded with a skeptical look. He rose and grabbed an overcoat, which he tossed to me, then put another on himself. "Follow me. And try not to get lost."

I scrambled to my feet, stuffing the last of the

cheese into my mouth, before hopping out the door on one foot and trying to put the overcoat on at the same time. I paused and grabbed some supplies, stuffing them into my pocket before following Machiavelli out the door. So far, I'd been twenty-four hours in the past on a quest to fix the relationship between my boss and his wife, and no one was dead, dying, or maimed. I had no technology, no running water, no glasses and no idea what I was doing. I think things were off to a fairly good start.

CHARLOTTE and her journalist friend met us outside the Medici main palazzi—what the very rich people called their houses, apparently. It was more than three times the size of Machiavelli's house and far more extravagant. Charlotte wore a long shirt over mens' hose and some sort of tunic thing that looked like it came from Scotland, and the journalist author lady— she needed a nickname, because I really wasn't going to call her The Author—wore something a little bit more normal for women of the time: a dress with all the appropriate frills and folds and things I knew nothing about. At least, she looked normal. Ish. Charlotte's giant sword was still strapped across her back, though I had a feeling this would not necessarily go over well with the people we were going to meet.

"Why did you bring this person with you?" Charlotte asked, pointing at Machiavelli. He took the accusation in stride and simply held up his hands, yawning.

"I was brought along because Cal Thorpe is exceedingly poor at direction, and because you all seem to be inclined to get into rather a serious amount of trouble. As I like to make a point of knowing what goes on in my city, it seemed only prudent to come along." Machiavelli looked at Charlotte with a wan smile. The Author—curses she was going to be called Mary—raised an eyebrow.

"Everyone, this is Niccolò Machiavelli. Niccolò, this is Charlotte the Unkillable and her strange writer friend, known as The Author. I've decided to call her Mary." I gestured to each person at the introduction, and all three fell silent, staring in disbelief.

"Machiavelli?!" Charlotte demanded, her hand twitching in the direction of her sword.

"The Unkillable?" Machiavelli asked, looking Charlotte up and down like she was some strange piece of modern art.

"Mary?!" Mary spluttered, glaring at me. "There was nothing wrong with my—"

"I wasn't going to call you The Author. If we get into trouble, I'm not going to yell out 'The Author, run!' So you get to be Mary. And if you don't like it, you are welcome to offer an alternative," I said, effectively shutting down all lines of questioning between all three of them. Charlotte stared, Machiavelli looked impressed, and Mary frowned. But they all seemed to get along well enough.

Charlotte huffed and turned towards the entrance of the extremely large stone building. It seemed to be a collection of rooms around a central courtyard, with a delicately dripping fountain in the middle. Don't ask me how it worked, because honestly I hadn't even expected them to have running water. The stones in this building were well polished and gleaming. Compared to the rest of the city, this was an extremely wealthy neighbourhood.

Charlotte took the lead, marching straight into the courtyard. Mary and Machiavelli followed behind her, leaving me to bring up the rear. I took one last look over my shoulder at the setting sun behind us and figured that this was a really bad idea. Unfortunately, it was the only idea we had.

Charlotte banged her fist on the door, not moving away as it sprang open and revealed a man wearing some sort of leather arming jacket and carrying a thin sword. The armour was far better quality than what I had worn the night before at my city guard post, and I got the impression that this person actually knew how to use that sword. Though, compared to Charlotte's massive blade, I doubted it would do much damage.

However, I was eminently capable of being stuck with a sword, so I figured I'd avoid a confrontation.

"Identify yourselves," the man said, putting his hand on the hilt of his blade. Charlotte opened her mouth to respond and I decided that this was perhaps more my territory than hers. I pushed past Mary and Machiavelli and stood beside Charlotte.

"I am Cal Thorpe and these are my companions, the lady Charlotte, her…maidservant Mary, and Niccolò Machiavelli, a well-known writer and scribe. We wish to speak with your masters, the Medici. And, before you inform us that it is in fact quite late for such a meeting, please tell them that we would prefer this remain more discrete. Our business does not necessarily involve the people who walk the streets of Florence, but the ones who work beneath the surface," I said, pulling out every fancy vowel in my repertoire and doing my best to sound like I knew what I was talking about. I didn't. The last time I had managed an audience with the vampires, they had kidnapped me because of my skill at marketing.

The guardsmen looked at me like I was a little crazy. I really hoped that whatever magic Time had used to make my words translate properly worked with subtle requests. Otherwise I was just going to have to come out and say something blatantly rude about blood drinkers. Given that we were trying to be discrete, going around shouting "vampire" would cause a good deal of panic. That would be unfortunate.

The guard growled for a moment, but jerked his head in an angry nod and then retreated back into the maze of buildings around the courtyard. He slammed the door behind him, preventing us from following. I looked at Charlotte and she frowned down at me. "I was going to introduce us. Demand entry. You didn't need to interrupt with your ridiculous word-twisting request. They won't see us if you talk like that," she said flatly.

"Trust me, this is much better than breaking down their door. Relations with people, making sure that our best foot is forward and that people see the image we wish them to see, that is my specialty. You don't want to meet with these people after having broken their door. They will take it out of your hide," I explained.

Machiavelli looked at me with the equivalent of the arms-folded-skeptic look that I usually got from Death when I said something particularly human.

"And how would you know so much, Cal Thorpe? After all, you have supposedly been out in the world for a very long time, supposedly so far out that you have no idea of our customs or our way of dress or anything. Yet you are, surprisingly at ease and claiming you know the best way to talk to the likes of the Medici."

I winced. I had become so accustomed to dealing with the supernatural in the last year or so that I had forgotten what it was like to be normal. What it was to conceal your identity and have to worry about people burning you or stabbing you with pitchforks because you were running around screaming "magic!" I had to remember that while I was nearly five hundred years in the past, I was also dealing with people who had no idea what was going on. And some who did. The trouble was differentiating between the two.

I was standing with a half-giantess at my side, flanked by a time traveling journalist with a massive ego. I was about to walk into a den of vampires. And I was bringing a normal, mortal, probably important historical figure. This was going to end really badly.

"Let's just say that I've dealt with similar situations in the past," I said, giving the best, vaguest explanation I could. Machiavelli opened his mouth to question me about such situations and the door opened, revealing not the guard but a person I assumed was a servant. I assumed this because there were two tiny puncture marks on his neck just above his collar. I wouldn't have seen them if I hadn't been looking for them, but I was about to walk into a den of beings that lived off the life-force of others. It made sense that those who worked in the household of a vampire probably were more food than servant. So I was paying attention to the details.

"My lords will meet with you now," the man said, sniffing and glaring down his nose at us. He stepped aside and let us walk past. Charlotte was large enough that she took up the entire doorway. By comparison, I felt very small. Especially when the door closed behind us with a heavy thunk of wood and I got a glimpse of the grandeur of the inside.

Besides being made from seriously well-crafted stone, the building was decorated with the finest Renaissance art and objects that I had ever seen. The splendour was obvious, ridiculous, and really, really splendid. I wanted to pull out my phone and snap some pictures, just to have proof that I had stood in a room with all these masterpieces. I almost did, until I remembered where we were.

These people, even if they were hiding behind a human name, were powerful with a very, very wealthy base. And they didn't need weapons to kill us.

The servant led us through an outer entrance hall and into a large dining area. The table was made of solid wood, with chairs in dazzling upholstery. The table was set with plates and plates of food, with some sort of primitive fork and a really sharp knife taking the primary place of the cutlery. All of the people sitting around the table were dressed in the style of the time, only with the nicest velvet fabrics and silk embroidered with fantastic designs. The clothes were obviously well made, and perfectly tailored. But, as I had expected, everything was just ever so slightly off.

The colours clashed with their skin. Their hairstyles were well done, but with strands sticking straight out or in the wrong spot. They were wearing the best, but with that lack of perfect style that all vampires seemed to have. It was a result of their inability to look at themselves in the mirror. I imagine that most of these vampires were dressed by other people, which accounted for the fact that they were slightly better put together than the modern counterparts. Vampires were also petty enough to not tell each other when they looked a little funny. It was some sort of weird power play that I didn't quite understand.

An older gentleman—gentlevamp?—sat at the head of the table, looking to be about his mid forties, though I knew that age was more or less irrelevant to these creatures. To his left sat a beautiful matriarch, whom I recognised as Thaddeus's mother, Alsatia. At his right, Thaddeus himself. He gestured to our group, beckoning us to come a little bit forwards into the room. We were not offered a seat at the table.

"You said you had business dealings to discuss. Discrete business dealings. Tell me why I should listen to what you have to say when you so rudely interrupted our evening meal," the patriarch said. I looked around and saw no evidence of human presence except for the servant who now stood off to one side. Nor did it appear that they were actually eating anything.

Charlotte looked at me, waiting for me to say something, eyebrows raised. I shrugged and shook my head. "You're the one who wanted a meeting," I whispered.

Charlotte huffed. She straightened her shoulders and stepped forward. "I am Charlotte the Unkillable. I have come seeking the Eye of Carteria. My resources have informed me that it is in your possession."

Wow. Charlotte really needed to work on her business strategy. These people would never respond like that. And, moments later, I was proven right. The patriarch exchanged a glance with Thaddeus, then threw back his head and laughed. "Even if we did have this Eye that you seek, why in the world would we give it to you? Even if you were to purchase it, the price would be beyond your means."

Then, Charlotte did something incredibly stupid. She drew the massive sword from its sheath across her back and levelled it in two hands, the tip directly pointing at the vampire patriarch. In an instant, the vampires were on their feet. I, perhaps being as stupid as Charlotte, leapt in front of her sword and held my hands up. "Are you crazy?!" I demanded.

Machiavelli, who was now pressed against a wall, his eyes wide, nodded. "I would say yes," he said. Mary just shrugged.

"Actually, I'm used to this. She's being fairly restrained. There was this one time that we were trying to get into some caves in Tibet, only they were being guarded and I didn't have any shoes and—"

Charlotte hissed at her companion, though her eyes were fixed straight ahead. Her sword did not waver. Mary sighed dramatically, but kept quiet.

I glared at Charlotte and Mary, holding out my hands to try and prevent Charlotte from killing anybody or them killing her. "Do you know, this isn't very helpful," I said. Risking my back, I turned and faced the vampires who were all staring at us, hissing low in their throats. "Honestly, she just said she wanted some sort of artefact. I didn't know that it would involve massive pointy swords. Just for the sake of our lives, would you terribly mind if we asked what it would cost to get this I thing?"

Thaddeus pointed at me, and I swore I could see a claw growing as he did. "Your insolence will cost you your life."

I shrugged. "Meh. I've been threatened with that before, by other vampires. It didn't stick."

You'd think I had just killed someone's cat by the way the entire room stared at me. No one said a word, and I swear I heard every heartbeat as loud as drums inside my head. The patriarch hissed at me, fangs gleaming in the candlelight. "You dare reveal us. You know what we are."

I looked around and saw Machiavelli staring with his jaw hanging open. Honestly I had no idea if the word vampire even meant anything to him, but given the look of shock on his face, I had to imagine that it did. Or that the translation that was being provided explained things very clearly. I would have to explain things to him later and hope that I hadn't broken history. There were other pressing matters just then, though.

I turned back to the vampires. "Well, yes. You're rather easy to spot. There is a certain je ne c'est quoi that all vampires possess. Something to do with image and style?"

Charlotte coughed behind me and I glanced over my shoulder. She was trying to keep a straight face, but her sword was bobbing in time with the tremors in her shoulders. I realised a moment later that she was *laughing*. I scowled. I turned back to the vampires and saw Thaddeus take a single step forwards.

"You have forfeit your lives, human. You will all die."

"Yeah, you know what. People have done that to me too, it didn't stick then either," I said. Then, I reached into the pocket on my coat and pulled out the supplies that I had stolen from Machiavelli's house. There weren't a lot of things that could take down a fully grown, well-fed vampire. Sunlight was good if you could get it, but as long as they were well covered, most vampires weren't bothered by it. Wooden stakes were nice, but it required special wood. Garlic though… garlic was something else entirely. I held a large bulb in either hand, showing them off to my vampire friends.

Thaddeus coughed and retreated that single step. The vampire patriarch hissed, this time more audibly. The woman, Alsatia, whose name had too many doggy connotations for me to *not* snigger, held her hands at her side and closed fists. "You dare," she said.

"Yes. I dare," I said. "Now, if you don't want me breaking this apart and lobbing it at you, I would suggest that you tell us what it is this Eye thingy would cost. Then we will be out of your hair until we have gathered the funds and can return. No harm, no foul. Capice?"

All three of the vampires narrowed their eyes. I waited. I could feel Charlotte shifting behind me, that sword slipping through the air like a hot knife through butter. Mary and Machiavelli, thank goodness, were silent. After what felt like an eternity, the patriarch spat on the ground. "The Eye will cost one blood debt. If you want it, you will have to kill somebody for us. Savonarola."

None of us reacted except Machiavelli, who coughed. I looked at Charlotte, who nodded. "It is time to leave now," she said, neither accepting nor refusing the demand. I had sort of hoped she would just immediately say no; I didn't really want to have to assassinate someone. I worked for Death. That didn't mean I killed people.

We retreated, me holding out the garlic until we were well clear of the maze of buildings. Charlotte kept her sword unsheathed until we were even farther down the street. We both put our respective weapons away, then turned to each other. Machiavelli shook his head, trembling slightly.

"This is bad," he said. At least he wasn't catatonic on the ground. One human I'd accidentally revealed things to had done just that. Another had tried to get my boss to take his memories. Machiavelli, except for the tremble in his hands, seemed to be relatively okay.

"Oddly enough, I've had worse," I said. Mary and Charlotte exchanged a glance.

Charlotte opened her mouth to say something when the world shifted. Excepting the four of us, everything became hazy. And not just the sort of hazy that came with not wearing my glasses. This was a true fog, ash dark and insidious. The world seemed to stop around us, every slight movement fading into nothingness, every sound becoming muted and dull. Everyone except me looked around as though the world had fallen from beneath their feet. I think Mary was going to scream, but she held it in. For me, I had experienced this before. So I just pulled out my glasses, perched them on my nose, and looked around for the person that I knew was coming our direction.

He appeared, tall and lean, darker than the blackest night, wearing the finest clothing that this time had to offer. His steps were calm and measured. "I felt the world shift as I wandered it, and I had to find out precisely who or what was the cause. Instead I found you four."

"Hello Death," I said with a smile.

Death tilted his head, looking at me with those empty eyes. "Do we know each other?"

"Oh yeah," I said. "We know each other."

A thought occurred to me before I could make the introductions and clear up a whole lot of confusion. I held up one hand and pushed up my glasses with the other. "Hold on. None of us has been seriously injured or, well, are close to dying. So what are you doing here? You shouldn't be able to pull us from the real world like that."

Death quirked his brow. "If you must know, you walked away from what should have been certain death. I don't like it when people do that."

I blinked. Actually, that made perfect sense. I shouldn't have been surprised that my terrifying boss had more tricks up his sleeve than I knew, but he always managed to do that. I didn't even want to know what tricks Life had up her sleeve.

"Okay," I said with a shrug. Charlotte and Machiavelli turned on me. Charlotte was glaring and Machiavelli was staring, open-mouthed like a fish. Mary had managed to fish out her scroll and was scribbling again, not actually looking at us but paying far too much attention. Death watched her with mild interest, which was a bad thing.

"Okay?" Charlotte demanded. "Okay?! We were pulled from the world by *Death* and you just shrug it off?"

I pointed at Death. "Well, he is my boss, remember?"

Charlotte growled. Death looked surprised. Machiavelli broke out spluttering.

"He is?"

"I am?"

I sighed. This was going to require more than a few minutes' worth of explanation. I looked around for some place to maybe sit and discuss this, like Death had done for me on a park bench in the middle of the city park, after I'd been shot. He had pulled me from the world in the Instant of Death and offered me a job. I still remembered the blind panic that had nearly overtaken me. Actually, much of the first week was spent in a blind panic. So frankly, Charlotte's reaction didn't surprise me. Nor did Machiavelli's. Mary's, though, seemed to be a little weird. What did I know about writers or journalists, though? Maybe that was her way of coping.

I didn't spot a place to sit so instead I tried to put my hands into my pockets, only to discover that I wasn't wearing pockets. I rested my hands on my belt instead.

"So, here's how everything works. About a year ago,

you—" I pointed to Death, "found me in a park and offered me a job as your public relations manager. Only, you don't know that you did this because that was, ah, will be, several hundred years from now. Anyways, I got pulled back through time by Time and ended up here, where I came upon you—" I pointed to Machiavelli, whose fish impression had improved, "who helped me figure out what the heck is going on. Then you two—" Charlotte and Mary exchanged a glance, "showed up and we struck a bargain to fetch some ridiculous artefact from a den of vampires. Now here we are, rehashing things that haven't happened yet. Have I left anything out?"

Death tilted his head and examined me top to bottom, like I was an interesting specimen. Frankly, it was a little unnerving. "Really? I offered you a job? As my public...*relations* manager?"

"Yep," I said. Then I paused. "Wait. No. Relations doesn't mean what you think it means. I mean, it does, just...You know what? Never mind."

"No, no, this is all very interesting," Death said, smiling. It was a familiar smile, one that I had seen several times before. The only problem was, I had only ever seen that particular manic smile on his wife, Life. She was the one who seemed to enjoy crazy situations and making trouble for people. She was the one who revelled in the chaotic and smiled at people like that, as if they were there for her amusement and entertainment. "I am fascinated. It seems so implausible, and yet somehow makes sense. Luckily for you, there is a way to prove your story correct. If I have truly offered you a job in the future, then I would have done this."

Before I could react, Death reached out and touched me on the forehead. Now, for a normal human, this would have been bad. Death would have killed them immediately. I'd seen it done, on Justice, an air elemental gone rogue. For me? Well, the first time Death had done that, he made a mistake that had made me impossible to kill. The second time, he had supposedly fixed that mistake. Not that I'd bothered to test that theory, mind you. I had no idea what would happen when he touched me a third time.

In any case, it didn't really matter. I was too busy screaming with pain that overwhelmed the senses to worry too much about it. Like it had twice before, the world around me vanished into nothing but overwhelming agony. My vision blanked out, my ears rang, my fingers curled. I could tell, faintly, that my heart was beating rapidly, but I did not know if that was a good thing. Someone could have been hacking my limbs off and I would not have noticed it, so all encompassing was the pain.

Then, just as suddenly as it began, it stopped.

I gasped for air, my lungs heaving as I tried to fill them. My muscles weakened and I fell to my knees. Gradually, I became aware of my surroundings again. I saw Charlotte standing between Mary and Death, her hand on her sword. She looked murderous, but I saw a sheen of sweat on her brow. Machiavelli was off to one side, vomiting into the street. And Death was watching me curiously, looking a little shocked.

I reached up and touched the spot where Death had touched me. The skin was smouldering a little, and my fingers came away hot. I touched the spot again and the wound had apparently healed. I groaned and sat back against a stone wall opposite the Medici palazzi. "Do you know, I really, really wish you wouldn't do that. You *or* Life. It sucks more than you can imagine."

"Ah," Death said, voice flat and far more like the Death I was used to. The sensible, think-things-through Death. "This could be a problem."

"A problem?" I snapped. "I would say so. That hurt!"

"I imagine it did," Death said. He crouched before me and examined me with those empty pits that served as eyes. I fancied I saw a flicker of light somewhere in the depths, but I did not want to look too closely. "Your soul has been severed."

"Again?" I sighed. Really, this was getting frustrating.

"Again? Ah, I see…It is different this time," Death said. "Why did you not tell me that you had received my touch twice before?"

"I would have, if you'd let me *explain* things before going all 'oh, let's touch Cal and see what happens' on me. Sheesh! I did *not* sign up for this. When I get back to the future, I'm going to renegotiate my contract." I rubbed my forehead again. Charlotte had gone to help Machiavelli, but was still watching me with interest. Mary had not once ceased scribbling on her scroll, her eyes darting between the scene before her and the paper, as though trying to capture every detail. I reminded myself to burn those scrolls before this was done.

"If you had told me," Death said as though I hadn't said anything, "then perhaps I would have changed my approach. As it is, your soul has been severed."

"Yeah, you said that. Been there, done that. You fixed it before, you can do it again," I said, holding out my hand to Death and preparing for more pain. What I was not prepared for was Death to shake his head.

"I cannot. It is one thing to separate a person's soul from their lifeforce, their essence. It is another to sever a person from their soul. I cannot fix this, because your soul is no longer here," Death said. I frowned, trying to put logic behind these words. What logic stuck had my heart stopping in horror.

"You *lost it?!*" I screamed. "You lost my soul!"

Death stood and, in the most human gesture I had ever seen him make, shrugged. I was suddenly struck with a great desire to throttle my boss. In fact, I was on my feet and halfway to Death when Charlotte held me back.

"Cal Thorpe, this will not end well. You cannot go against Death and win," she said.

"He lost my soul!" I wailed, struggling against Charlotte's arms around my waist and doing my best to get to Death.

"Yes," Charlotte said, as though she were agreeing about the weather. "He did."

"I want my soul back!" I fought against Charlotte, but it was like fighting against a boulder with a sword.

Pointless. "Who knows what's going to happen to me now!"

"There are some side effects," Death said, looking at the sculpture of a gargoyle on one of the palazzi and very pointedly not meeting my gaze. I wanted to wrap my hands around his neck and shake him. "I would not worry. It is extremely unlikely that you would ever experience most of them."

"I'm going to soak all of your neckties in bleach," I snarled. "I'm going to put ghost peppers in your tea. I—"

"Enough!" Charlotte snapped. "This is an unfortunate situation, but it does not change the reality of things. You are not dead. You are not dying. You merely have to go find your soul."

"Find my soul?" I asked incredulously, shock making me stop struggling. "Where? Heaven? Hell? Some unknown corner of the universe?"

"I do not know," Death said. He held up a slim finger as I opened my mouth to protest. "It is possible, though, that I will know."

"How?" I ground out. My fists were clenched at my side and I was feeling anything but calm and rational.

"You say that you work for me several hundred years into the future, no? Perhaps my knowledge has expanded then. Perhaps things have changed. You merely need to speak with me then," Death said. I said nothing for a moment, trying to get my breathing under control before I started screaming again.

"And how, *exactly*, would you suggest I do that? Are you going to transport me there?" I asked. My fists were clenched at my side. Mary's eyes widened and she grinned before scribbling faster. Machiavelli took a step backwards. Charlotte put a firm hand on my shoulder to keep me from doing anything stupid.

"No, that would require my cousin, Time," Death said simply. "Merely summon him as you did before and then ask him to take you forwards."

"I didn't summon Time before," I snapped. "He showed up at the stupid theatre! He initiated the stupid trip!"

"Ah, then I suggest you do what it was that he brought you here to do," Death said with an apologetic shrug. "I cannot say any more than that."

I pinched my nose between my fingers, practising every calm breathing technique I could remember. I finally let out a long, slow breath and looked up at Death, hoping that my anger and fear was burning a hole through his skull. "Time sent me here to help solve whatever relationship problems you and Life are having," I said with a malicious hiss.

Death blinked. Then smiled. "Then your task is already complete! My beautiful Life and I have no problems."

"Oh, really?" I asked. "Then where is she now?"

Death frowned. "Ah. I don't…"

"Exactly." I turned to Charlotte. "Okay, Charlotte. Here's the deal. I'll get you that artefact. You're going to help me with this imbecile. And Mary? Get Machiavelli before he falls and hurts himself."

"Imbecile?" Death asked, rolling the word around as

though he had never heard it applied to himself. "Interesting."

"Cal Thorpe, what are you going to do?" Charlotte asked in a worried tone. I took another deep breath.

"I'm going to go get a drink."

"So explain this to me again."

I looked up from where I was resting my head on the table, a goblet of wine in my hand, contemplating the liquid. Machiavelli looked at me over the rim of his own cup, well and truly on his way to being sozzled. Frankly, he was taking this far better than I would have thought.

"You arrived in Florence from the future because Time—the embodiment and entity that encompasses all that time represents—sent you back so that your master, Death, could reconcile with his wife, Life, before they became estranged as they are in the future? You managed to run into a wandering half-giantess and her scribe companion, who declared that they would help you in your task if you helped them with theirs. This task happened to be retrieving an artefact from the Medici, who are actually vampires—beings that drain the lifeblood from you—and you walked out of there in one piece, only to run into the Death from this time, who accidentally released your soul to who knows where. And the part that has you still a little shocked in all of this is that *I'm* meant to be some sort of politician?"

I drained the rest of my wine and immediately poured another. At this point, I had lost count of how much I had drank. I really didn't care, though. I was feeling unpleasantly un-drunk and really not thrilled about the whole situation.

"Some sort of *genius* politician-writer-type," I corrected absently. "But otherwise, that is entirely correct."

Machiavelli sank back into his seat and let out a breath. "I thought DaVinci was an unusual man, and he just invents flying machines."

I snorted in laughter. Machiavelli, who was considerably drunker than I was, joined me. We didn't stop laughing until Death himself came and sat at the table, Charlotte and Mary joining us and eyeing Death with wariness and unabashed interest respectively.

"If you touch someone, they die? But if you touch them more than once—" Mary was asking, her charcoal poised above her paper. She did not seem at all perturbed by the fact that Death was her interviewee.

"Where did you find these characters, Cal Thorpe?" Death asked, eyeing Mary uncertainly. I lifted my head.

"They found me," I said. "Actually, that's how most of the problems start. It's not like I ask for these things to happen. They just do. My job sucks."

"You do have an unusual proclivity towards chaos," Death agreed. I looked at him, taking in the clothes that looked like they belonged in a Shakespeare play, then looked back at the wine.

"Thanks, I guess," I grumbled. "Now here's a question: why aren't I drunk?"

Death grinned, the look far more maniacal than I liked. "Ah, now there is one of the more entertaining aspects of having a soul run amok. Some things you will feel stronger than before, for nothing filters it. You won't feel other things nearly as deeply as you would otherwise. Which means you can drink a whole lot more and not get drunk. Your soul, wherever it is, is likely feeling quite intoxicated, but will not, generally, suffer the aftereffects."

I raised my eyebrows. "Right. So basically my soul will be drunk—or hurt, or tired, or whatever—but I won't? I see where the idea for Dorian Grey came from."

"Stop feeling sorry for yourself!" Charlotte demanded, pounding her fist on the table. The wine jug and the assorted stoneware goblets jumped and fell with a clang. Machiavelli rescued the wine and I watched my cup fall to the floor. I pushed my glasses up and then realised that I was still wearing the stupid things. In public. In 1494. With normal humans around. I sighed and pulled them off, putting them into the same belt purse that held my phone. I touched the metal object and found some slight comfort in knowing that things would be better. Eventually.

"Didn't you hear Death?" I asked, gesturing to my boss. "I can't feel—"

"You or your soul, whatever. You are sulking. Sulking will not solve your problem," Charlotte said. She reached over the table and jabbed me in the chest. "Action is the only solution."

Mary nodded. "She has a point. I mean, when she

first found me, I was a snivelling, terrified weasel on the verge of an emotional breakdown. But here I am, with the makings of one of the best stories in centuries."

"Publish a word and I'll sue you," I grumbled. I didn't know what time Mary was from, but the words seemed to have some effect. She frowned, then grumbled and finally put her writing materials away.

I sighed, took a deep breath, tried to feel the sense of calm that normally came with such a thing, and felt nothing. Soulless. Right. It seemed to take some sort of great effort to push those thoughts aside, but I managed it. I sat up straight. I poured myself another glass of wine and savoured the flavour more than the need to get drunk. I closed my eyes, took another breath, and opened them.

"Okay, fine. So what do we need to do?" I said.

Charlotte nodded firmly. "Good. You are thinking straight again."

"I wouldn't say that. I'm not sure I've done *that* for a while, but I am going to fix this whole problem," I said, unable to suppress a glare at Death. He just watched me, empty eyes taking in everything as though I were uncharted territory, a mystery to be solved. A game. "You can't help me until I get back to the future—some sort of copyright infringement going on with that, but still. You'll have the information in the future."

Death inclined his head. "I will do my best to discover a means of fixing this."

I nodded. "Right. And you—" I pointed at Charlotte,

"are still determined to help me if I help you get that thing from the Medici."

"We found Death by that means," Charlotte said with a warrior's grin. "Surely we can find Life similarly."

"That's a terrifying thought, but likely accurate. So we get the artefact, find Life. I get you two to kiss and make up—"

"I should like to protest that there is nothing actually wrong with our relationship," Death said, raising a gentle finger. I replied with a skeptical eyebrow and he sighed. "Yes, very well. Time told you there was a problem between us here and now, so something must be done. Though I could not imagine what."

"Time said that you missed some terribly important appointment. And then that Life wouldn't let you get involved in some mortal person's end of days," I said. Death considered, frowning.

"I do not know what appointment my cousin refers to," Death said. I sighed and pinched the bridge of my nose.

"That's what I was afraid of," I said. At this point, I discovered that the jug of wine was empty and neither Charlotte nor Machiavelli were terribly forthcoming with money for more. As I had only just earned a tiny amount of money, I didn't think that wasting it on wine would be a worthwhile use of my time. Not to mention I wasn't actually feeling drunk, so that plan went out the window as well. Instead, I sighed and rested my chin on my fist. "Is there any way that you could, oh, I don't know, call Time up and get him to send me back?"

Death tilted his head. "I do not know this 'call' that you speak of. Do you wish me to shout?"

"No," I said, groaning. I had known that I wasn't in the time where I belonged, but this just hit home. Death—my boss, a familiar figure and all that—was not the Death I knew. I was stuck in a place that was technologically extremely different, full of people I didn't know, and a world that had already done worse than kill me. I had thought that the world of Elsewhere with all its magic, all its strangeness and danger, was terrible enough. I had wanted nothing more than to return to my normal life. I wanted to do marketing. Social media. *Normal* things. Now, I longed for even the strangeness of a few days ago. I pushed the empty jug away from me and rested my head on the table. Maybe sleep would provide me some relief.

"It seems to me," Machiavelli said, speaking up for the first time since Death, Charlotte and Mary had joined us, "that the best way to solve your problem is to learn more about the people involved."

I raised my eyebrows and looked up at him. "Oh?"

"You need to get an artefact from the Medici. Therefore, it would be useful to know what motivates them. What you can do to manipulate them in a direction that would be beneficial for you. They wish you to kill Savonarola, which would be tantamount to war on the lower classes of Florence, with the Church in the middle. So, in essence, they wish you to either give up, start a war, or figure out a different way of stealing this artefact. The Medici are powerful. They have influence in almost every quarter of this city. So why would they wish for you to kill such an important figure, with influence in the Church?" Machiavelli asked. I blinked and glanced over at Charlotte.

I had forgotten about the ridiculous request the Medici had made in all the hullaballoo that followed. Losing your soul does tend to make you forget a few things. But, we had to start somewhere to fix this, and the best place was the artefact that Charlotte wanted. I took in a deep breath to focus myself. I thought I felt the same as I normally did, but Death had said that things would be different without my soul. So maybe I needed to push myself a little more to focus. Alright, fine. I took another deep breath.

"Okay, so the Medici are trying to use us as a scapegoat. They either want to start this war without anyone knowing that it was them who started it, or they really don't think we're going to do it, in which case they don't really want the war to start. But… why would they make such a ridiculous request if there is even the slightest chance that we would do it?"

Machiavelli flapped his hand dismissively. "No one is stupid enough for that."

I snorted. "Trust me, people are a whole lot stupider than you think they are."

Death chuckled, shaking his head. "Humans are such an unusual species. No matter how much time I spend amongst you, you are always surprising me. Perhaps that is why I brought you into my service centuries from now, Cal Thorpe."

I banged my fist on the table, making everyone in the tavern jump. Silence fell and I had to work hard not to shout. I was breathing heavily, anger coursing through my veins, stronger the longer I tried to control it. "Alright. First off, it's Cal. Just Cal. No Cal Thorpe. No Calvin. Just Cal. Got it?"

"Got it," Mary squeaked. Charlotte nodded, but her gaze had hardened and her hand was reaching towards her sword.

Death blinked languidly. "You humans may be unusual, but do not forget that you are just that. Human. Fragile. Do not presume to make such demands to me."

I snapped.

I turned to face Death head on. Baring my teeth like I had seen plenty of immortal beings do—sylphs, rock trolls, vampires, you name it—I leaned in close enough so that Death could feel my breath on his face. "I'll make whatever demands I want. Do you know why? Because I'm not human anymore. You can't harm me. You *made* me."

The shadows lengthened. Light seemed to just evaporate into mist. The world around me slowed until even my breath seemed to hang in mid-air. Death's power pulsed, making him the centre of the world, of *my* world, until it was impossible to look away. I could see his power leeching into the table, into the wine, into Machiavelli and Charlotte and Mary. I could see it inching closer to me, until it stopped, tantalisingly close.

Part of me longed to reach out and touch it. I

wanted to see what would happen. I wanted to see if contact with that undeniable force would take me to bliss, or if it would do nothing at all.

"I am the Inevitable," Death said, his voice deep enough that my whole body vibrated with the sound. "No matter what you have become, you *will* face me in the end. Nothing escapes me. Nothing at all. I am the horror of civilisations. I am the nightmare in everyone's head. I am the last and the enduring."

The power seemed to fade, until Death was looking at me and holding my attention not through intimidation or fear, but because his empty eyes held a glimmer of kindness. "I have done grievous harm in rupturing the connection to your soul, but I will seek a solution to this. Until then, you may be impossible to kill, but you are not impossible to change. Be wary."

I nodded, blinking away moisture from my eyes. Whatever anger I had was gone. Now, there was nothing but pain that I couldn't even feel. It was like the pain, the horror and sorrow lay behind a thick veil. I knew it was there. It tormented me. But I could only see it—feel it—out of the corner of my eye.

Death reached out and, tentatively, patted my shoulder. I smiled weakly and turned back to the others. They looked away, saying nothing.

"What is this artefact that you are so interested in?" Death asked Charlotte conversationally. Her breath caught in her throat, but she shook off whatever fear or strangeness she felt and answered. It was as though, after seeing the terror of Death, everything was too normal.

"The Eye of Carteria," Charlotte said. Mary nodded eagerly. Machiavelli looked at me and I shrugged. But Death? He tilted his head back and laughed. The sound was loud enough to rattle the walls, much to the astonishment of the other patrons.

"The Eye of Carteria?" Death asked, wiping moisture from an eye. "You are either insane, or you live up to your moniker, Charlotte the Unkillable."

"Would someone like to explain to me what is going on?" I asked. "What is the Eye of Carteria?"

Death looked at me and gave a quiet hum. He drummed his fingers on the table and then turned back to Charlotte. "Would you like to explain, or shall I?"

Charlotte blinked. But before either Death or Charlotte could say a word to enlighten me on what the heck was going on, Mary dumped a scroll on the table and rolled it open, holding it flat with the empty wine jug and my empty cup. She coughed and brushed her skirt like she was getting ready for a meeting. She pointed to a sketch of an amulet thing. It had eight sides and a single jewel in the centre, shaped like the slit in a wyvern's eye. It was surrounded by tiny glyphs in a language I didn't recognise.

"This is the Eye of Carteria," Mary said proudly. Machiavelli leaned over the paper and frowned, but it appeared this enlightened him no more than me.

"I don't get it," I said.

Mary looked at our blank expressions and huffed. "Does *no one* do proper research anymore? No, they just expect the journalist or the writers to do if for them!"

"So, Charlotte, this Eye is—"

"Would you just listen to me?!" Mary snapped, her face turning an amusing shade of red. She then pointed to a paragraph of writing just below the drawing. "The Eye of Carteria is a legend said to have existed at the beginning of the Elsewhere. It supposedly helped the shaping of Elsewhere into what it is, separating the magical realms from the mortal realms. It took the dreams of people about what magic was like and shaped it into a world where magic could run free. In essence, the sorcerer who owned the Eye created the biggest and baddest prison in existence. To contain not just magical beings, but beings like Life and Death themselves, or dragons who are older than dirt and more powerful than just about—"

Death raised a hand and Mary halted, scowling. "The important piece of information is that the Eye is a powerful artefact. It contains and it separates. The power that this artefact holds is immense and it cannot be utilised by someone who does not have will to match its potential. Many people in the past have tried to wield the Eye with poor result."

"Why?" Machiavelli asked. Death, Charlotte, and Mary blinked at him, as though he had said something ridiculous.

"Why what?" Charlotte asked.

"Why would you want to wield it? I mean, what would that do?" Machiavelli asked. He inclined his head to Death. "Besides kill you, that is."

Mary huffed and folded her arms. "If a person managed to successfully wield the Eye of Carteria, then they would have power over Elsewhere. And magical beings."

"For an author, you're not terribly informative," I huffed back at Mary. Her eyes widened in fury and she jabbed her finger at a piece of the scroll, farther down the page than the drawing.

"You've already experienced something like what the Eye can do," Mary snapped, perhaps far too loudly for the other patrons of the tavern. "Your *soul* was cleaved from your person. You were separated at a level so essential, so basic, that even Death himself cannot undo this mistake. Imagine if you could do that to anyone. If you could separate a dragon's magic from them and then contain it. Use it. Or if you could contain the greatest threats to the world. If you could cleave and contain *anything*."

Silence fell at the table. Machiavelli made a considering noise in his throat, then sipped at the wine still in his glass. "An interesting question. I know many who would gladly take such power and use it for their own purposes, rather than what it was intended to do. The question is, what are you planning to do with it?"

Charlotte's expression hardened. She shifted in her seat, reaching towards a weapon that was probably hidden in her belt. "You presume to ask me such a question?"

Machiavelli raised his brows. "I presume to ask. Why? Because you have gotten me involved in this situation." Charlotte opened her mouth to complain and Machiavelli replied by holding up his hand for silence. "Yes, I am fully aware that you were given no choice in my involvement. But the fact of the matter is that I am now involved. And it seems to me that I should know what your intentions are for such a dangerous artefact. I am not going to help release some sort of demon upon the earth."

"She's not a demon!" Mary protested. Charlotte rolled her eyes and shook her head.

"Actually, I think Niccolo has a point," I said, straightening. "I know more than a few beings whose power would be really, really devastating if used at someone's whim. Like him." I jerked my thumb towards Death who simply shrugged.

"Such artefacts are powerful, yes. Dangerous, yes. But Life and I chose to enter the realm of Elsewhere. We are not contained by such puny objects," Death said. He smiled into his own drink, looking back at me with a smug expression. I didn't return the smile.

"Do you know my purpose in life?" Charlotte asked.

"Oh, goodie! The story! Can I tell it?" Mary asked, clapping her hands and looking around with an expression of glee.

"No," Charlotte snapped. "If you wish to call yourself The Author, no matter that it is supremely ridiculous, fine. But every time you tell this story you twist everything I've done into something... else."

Mary shrugged, looking unconcerned by the accusation. "It is my job. I take the kernel of truth at the centre of anyone's story and bring it to the front. It is not my fault if people don't like the result."

"Enough!" Charlotte growled. "I will tell my own story."

She turned to Machiavelli, leaning forwards and wrapping her hands around the empty glass. I had a feeling that this was more for a way to control her hands than anything else. "I was ostracised from birth by being what I am. There was nothing I could do. The giants would not have me for being weak and the humans would not have me for being strong. I was powerful, yes, but not powerful enough to gather attention or respect. Just enough to be considered an oddity. So I decided that I would gather power. I went searching for things that could grant me power. I learned how to wield the greatsword on the way. I faced ogres and wyverns and furious immortals. I fought my way through the human lands and through Elsewhere. And I came upon several artefacts. Eventually, though, I discovered that respect was anything but forthcoming. There was no awe, no admiration. Only fear. Then, I kil—never mind...It doesn't matter. Just know that I learned there are consequences for our actions. Terrible consequences. I would never be anything but an oddity. Or feared. I decided I would rather have people look at me strangely than with fear. So I packed up the artefacts and took them to the Library at Sazhem. I've been hunting down the worst things this realm has to offer ever since. Making sure that they can never escape into the world. Never be the cause of more fear. More consequences."

Once again, silence descended. Charlotte's story was full of holes, but I had a pretty good idea of what had happened. Someone close to her, or even an innocent stranger, had died and if it wasn't directly her fault, it was her fault by indirect means. It was something I had seen before and, given my line of work, would see again. Normally, I would have felt a surge of pity for her and would have trusted her to do what needed to be done then and there. But things were far from normal for me. I required answers.

I looked at Mary, at The Author, and asked: "Which will history see her as: the villain, or the hero?"

Mary scoffed. "Neither. If she does her job right, you won't see her at all. That's why she took the name Unkillable. You can't kill something that no one remembers."

"Stupid scribe," Charlotte muttered, but didn't argue.

"A touching story," Machiavelli said drily. "Just the sort to tug on our heartstrings and try to make us believe that you really are working for the greater good. I still don't trust you."

This time, Charlotte bared her teeth at Machiavelli. "Then don't. I enlisted Cal's help, not yours. Feel free to go back to your writing and scheming, tiny human."

I opened my mouth to argue and was, again, interrupted. Death let out another hum, his dark and empty eyes looking at something beyond what any of us could see. I felt a shadow passing over my mind and wondered if that was to do with my missing soul or if it was the hint of fear I couldn't feel anymore.

"How interesting that you particular people should be drawn together at this particular time. A human, made immortal. A half-giantess. A scribe, out of her own time. And a normal, fragile human with a gift of thought. Immortal, scion, adventurer, philosopher. All brought together to help one another retrieve one of the most powerful artefacts this realm has seen, then to supposedly help me in my troubles. Which then begs the question: who, in their right mind, would help Death? There is perhaps something more going on here. Something you are not seeing."

Death looked at each of us, focusing on us for a few interminable seconds before moving on. Once, that lingering gaze would have struck quivering terror right through me. Now, I frowned and sighed.

"A little dramatic, don't you think?" I asked. "If there is something else going on here, Time is the one you should be asking. He brought us here. Well, he brought me. And if he brought me here, then he did it on purpose. Okay, fine, he probably has ulterior motives. I really don't care; I just want to get back home and get my soul. So I'll go help Charlotte and Mary in their 'righteous' quest for the Eye. Then we need to make sure you get to your appointment on time. Got it?"

Death held out his hands in mock surrender. "Very well. But there is just one problem: I have thought about this a great deal and have come up with no answers. Life and I have no appointment. I wish you luck."

With a blink of light so faint that I doubted anyone else in the tavern saw it, Death vanished. This wasn't the dramatic scene of before, when he used his power to leech the life and energy from the party, but something different. One minute he was there, the next he was gone. I let out a huff and grumbled into my empty glass.

"Death is… more eccentric than I would have thought," Machiavelli said, staring at the spot where Death had sat.

"Yeah, well, you should meet Life. Of the two of them, she scares me more. Death may be unexpected, but at least he's sane. She's…different. Unpredictable. And what did he mean by he never made an appointment?!" The last I asked more to myself than anybody, but the others seemed to feel free to offer their own opinions.

"Maybe Death is correct," Machiavelli said. "Perhaps there is something else going on. Perhaps you were brought here as a means to a different end than the one you thought. Time does not seem the most stable entity, based on how you've described him."

I nodded, considering. "That is true."

"I say we continue with the plan," Charlotte said. "Help me retrieve the Eye."

"Then maybe we'll have enough pieces to figure out what's going on," Mary added, rolling up the documents she had spread out on the table and putting them back in her belt purse.

I took in a deep breath through my nose, then let it out slowly. It was a breathing technique that I had learned while doing yoga in the human realms. It used to work wonders for me, back when I was just about to become vice president of marketing in the PR firm where I worked. Now, it just served to fuel me with oxygen. "Alright. But I think we should go in a different direction after we get you that amulet. Instead of hoping that Death will help us figure out what I need to do to fix things with Life, I think we should talk to her instead."

"You just said that Life is incredibly unstable," Machiavelli pointed out. Mary agreed, soberly nodding, though I swore I saw a gleam of interest in her eyes.

"Yeah," I said. "I did. And she is. But the way my day is going, I'm up for a little unstable."

"Good," Charlotte said. "Then we rob the Medici at dawn."

Machiavelli choked on his drink.

"This is an incredibly stupid idea," I said under my breath as our ragtag group wandered through the darkened streets of Florence. Machiavelli was walking closest to me and gave me a glance, a glint in his eye that could have been either knowing or accusing.

"I thought you were separated from strong emotions. Would not such an opinion indicate strong emotion?" he breathed back. I shrugged, then shook my head as Charlotte—obviously in the lead, however reckless that might prove to be—strode through the narrow streets as though she owned them. Few would bother standing against her.

"It's not exactly separated," I said, tugging at the fit of my shirt. As soon as we started off on this thieving venture, it felt too tight, too much like a costume. Like I was a pretender. "It's more like everything I'm feeling, everything I am, is behind a thin veil. It is there; I know what it is and that it exists, but it doesn't affect me like it should. I can even ignore it, if I don't think about it. But that doesn't matter. I don't need to be able to feel emotion to know that this is an incredibly stupid idea."

"And yet here you are," Machiavelli said. He paused as a sleepy city guardsman walked past, nodding in acknowledgement to us. It was nearing dawn and we were lucky that the city hadn't yet started to stir. But our window of opportunity was waning. If we were going to stop and think about things, then it had to be before we started on this venture. Otherwise, we would never be able to get past the Medici again. We hadn't bothered with the planning or thinking, just leapt right into things. Hence the incredibly stupid idea.

"And yet here I am," I agreed. I took a deep breath and considered the two women leading us into danger. Charlotte strode sure and strong, her sword slung across her back as though she did not care that anyone knew she would be the one to beat, the dangerous one. Mary, on the other hand, was more subtle. She wore the clothing of a typical, average woman in that time. The only oddity was that her belt contained a bag of charcoal and another with paper. Her steps were careful, sure to pass only on solid stone rather than the mortar between. Her eyes watched and took in the details surrounding us. Of the two, Charlotte would be more likely to kill. Mary would simply tear someone apart from the inside out.

"I wonder why it is that you *are* here," Machiavelli

said quietly. I paused a moment, some strange feeling tugging at me from behind the veil. I focused and finally identified it by the sharp tang it left in my mouth. Uncertainty.

"To get their help in figuring out this whole situation with Life and Death," I said, swallowing away that uncertainty. It vanished back behind that veil as though I had never known what it was. That in itself was disconcerting. So I didn't have access to my emotions or whatever you wanted to call it. That didn't mean I was incapable of rational thought…did it?

"I wonder," Machiavelli said. At that, Mary turned around and shushed us.

We fell into silence and listened to the city start to wake up around us. False dawn was here and it was time for another day to start. Everyone would be going about their business, be that baking breads or preparing cloth. The vampires, though, would probably be just heading towards their beds. Yes, some few of them went out during the day to maintain the appearance of normality, but vampires were, on the whole, nocturnal. Their vaults would be vulnerable. Any humans hired to guard the vaults would likely be changing shift at that moment. Without modern technology like security cameras, motion sensors and the like, breaking into the Medici vault should have been as simple as slipping in, getting past the guards, and finding the artefact.

Of course, it wasn't really that simple.

Annoyed by our whispering, Mary hurried Machiavelli and I to the Medici palazzo. The courtyard was empty and calm. Charlotte put her ear to the door, as though she could hear something through the heavy wood. A thought occurred to me.

"Question," I whispered, raising my hand. All three of my companions turned towards me with alarm. "Why would the vault be here and not in their bank?"

"Hello! Magical artefact," Mary hissed. "Not something you'd leave lying about in a human bank."

I shrugged and hoped more than believed that to be true. The truth was, it was far easier to break into the palazzo than the bank. The consequences, though, would be much more dire.

Charlotte waved her hand in some sort of "all clear" then, hands hovering near her weapons and her feet stepping carefully so she didn't make noise on the stones, moved towards a door that led to the side of the palazzo. It was a servant's entrance, which didn't really make sense to me. The front would surely be the better way in. At this time of morning, the servants would be stirring, preparing the household for the day. Even stupid, modern me knew that.

That thought itched in my ear when before the severing of my soul it probably would have been something I'd thought of before now. At this point, I was on uncertain terrain with myself. I would have to trust that the others around me knew what they were doing so I could figure out how to sort out what I was thinking and not feeling. As we passed through the door leading to the servant's entrance, it occurred to me that trying to figure out my existential crisis on the fly while breaking into a nest of vampires was perhaps not the best idea.

So, I repeated once more, just as I was passing inside the palazzo, "This is an incredibly stupid idea."

No one chastised me for breathing the words out loud. Charlotte did take an almost audibly deep breath before continuing on into the depths of the stone building. That was not exactly encouraging.

There were fewer people about than I had expected. Perhaps because everybody was off doing work somewhere else in the household or in the city. Or, perhaps because the passages that we walked through fairly stank of that rancid vampire magic. They did not possess huge amounts of magic—the vampire royalty was accordingly better suited for magic than their subjects—but what they did possess was for enthralling. The aftereffect was something like a pastry that had gone off and smelled like burnt treacle. The passages we followed became narrower, more cobwebbed, and the smell of burnt treacle became stronger.

Until it stopped altogether.

Charlotte stepped into an open chamber with vaulted ceilings that seemed impossibly high. The palazzo could not be that large. I realised belatedly that we had been slowly descending into the depths of the earth. Each passage we took had been sloped down, lowering into the next passage, each step deceptive until you reached this enormous chamber and realised the depth of your mistake.

And it *was* a mistake.

The room was not, as I had expected, guarded by one or two soldiers, it was guarded by a single person. The female vampire, the future queen of the vampires that I had dealt with before and also threatened to kill —though thankfully she wouldn't know that for many hundreds of years. Alsatia. She lounged on a chair with elaborate embroidery as though she had nothing better to do with her time. As though she was expecting us.

When we all filed into the room, she grinned, showing off her fangs. "Ah," she said, eyes widening in the dim light. "You decided the price was too high to pay. So instead you are going to steal it."

Charlotte drew her greatsword, the metal rasping against its sheath and making it seem all the more ominous. I could see her profile and her teeth were drawn in a snarl with a hint of ferocious pleasure lingering there. Mary, too, was grinning like the thought of a battle pleased her. Machiavelli and I exchanged a glance and, as one, turned. It was too late. The entrance to the chamber behind us was being guarded by two ghouls. They would have been tall had not their bodies been hunched over. Their teeth gleamed in the torchlight, dripping in venomous drool. Their eyes flashed yellow with hunger. They took a single step forwards, claws rasping on the stone.

I heard the vampiress speak in the background, her attention taken with Charlotte. "Were you not enthralled with the prospect of fighting a war?"

"Fighting doesn't frighten me," Charlotte replied. Her feet scuffed on the floor and I imagined that she was stepping closer to her quarry. "Starting a needless war? No, even that doesn't frighten me. It does confuse me, though. Did you actually expect us to go through with it?"

Alsatia laughed, the sound grating. I winced and noticed that the ghouls did the same. Interesting. "That's not the point, my dear," she replied. There came a sound that was sharp and horrible, piercing my ears so that I instinctively drew my hands up to my ears and looked over my shoulder to see the vampiress dragging her claws across the stone, fangs bared in a giddy smile.

Looking away, though, would cost me.

Ghouls, you see, are not as dumb as they look. They look like mindless monsters interested only in their next meal and who are supremely capable at getting it. In reality, they could beat Yolanda at chess. (Granted, beating my assistant at chess is not a huge accomplishment, but still.) So when I turned my head to see what was making that horrible noise, they pounced.

The body of the slightly smaller one slammed into me, driving me into the floor. The larger ghoul was only a microsecond slower, but its claws were just as sharp. As the smaller ghoul's momentum carried it off of me, the larger sank its claws into my chest and its teeth reached for my throat. I yelped, before the sound was cut off. The pain was sharp and terrible, but it was nothing like what I had felt when Death touched me. The wounds were bad enough, though, to cause the edge of my vision to go dark.

In the background, I heard a scream—I was fairly

certain that it was Machiavelli, but the rage in that scream didn't make sense. I heard the vampire cackling, that sound completely familiar. And I heard the air part, probably as Charlotte's greatsword joined the battle. I heard the victory cry of the ghouls and then their strange laughter, like a reptile and a seagull had a child.

A few heartbeats later and the pain dissipated enough for me to move. I groaned and reached up to touch my throat, fairly certain what I would find. I was right, too. The flesh was torn to pieces, the edges ragged and bloody. In anybody else, the wound would have been fatal. But I worked for Death and had just lost my soul. Annoyingly, this had happened before. This time it was slightly different in that I didn't completely black out, but the main point was that I couldn't be killed.

It sucked. A lot.

I had to wait a few more seconds, even a minute, while my wounds healed enough for me to move around and stand. A lot can happen in a minute when you're fighting. This minute had brought about the decapitation of the larger ghoul—thank you, Charlotte—and the vampiress gaining a cut on her cheek. Mary and Machiavelli faced off against the smaller ghoul, Mary wielding a dagger and Machiavelli the thin rapier that he had tied to his belt before we started this crazy attempt. So we weren't completely out of the fight.

I groaned, this time on purpose and much louder, drawing the attention of the people we were fighting. Everybody froze.

"Cal Thorpe!" Charlotte exclaimed, her eyes lighting up. Mary's jaw fell open and even Machiavelli looked a little sick. I had a feeling my throat was still healing. "You are not dead!"

"Why aren't you dead?" Alsatia asked, eyes just as wide as everyone else's. It seemed that everyone was perfectly content to pause their desperate fight while I explained things. Even the ghoul, venom dripping onto the floor, didn't move towards me, instead hanging back with a confused expression.

"Ah, well…ow," I said, cracking my back. "I hate it when that happens."

"This has happened before?" Mary asked, sounding more like a curious journalist than a shocked companion. I shrugged.

"Well, the first time was when an angry Irishman cut my throat open. Then a vampire tried to drink my blood to enthral me and poofed—"

"Poofed?" the vampiress asked. I nodded.

"Poofed." I pushed my glasses farther up my nose and continued. "Then the Order of Silence tried to have me killed only to freak out when that didn't really work. It was a mistake on Death's part, when we shook hands to bind me to him—"

"You work for *Death*?" the vampire shrieked. I nodded again.

"I mean, I thought he had fixed it, but then this whole accidentally lost my soul bit happened and here we are again. Though it was different then. The pain lasted longer. Now, it's just like a mild ache. I mean, to be fair, the ache mostly happens when the wounds are trying to reknit themselves, but oh, well." I turned slowly around the room and fixed each and every person there in my gaze for a few seconds before ending with Charlotte and I staring at each other.

She was breathing hard, but not heavily, the gleam of adrenaline plain in her eyes and in the flush of her skin. If I didn't know better, I'd say she was enjoying this. Her hands shifted grip on the greatsword. "You cannot die."

"No," I said, holding my hands out to my side and knowing full well that I looked grim, covered in blood and bearing no wounds. "I cannot die."

Charlotte looked over her shoulder, addressing the future vampire queen. "Are you certain you wish to pursue this useless task? Guarding an artefact you cannot even wield against a man who can face Death and never lose?"

The only noise that followed was the rasping breath of the ghoul. Alsatia grew pale, which was surprising given her species. She brushed her hands on her dress and her claws retracted, as did her fangs. A few moments later and she was nothing more than a slightly-questionably-dressed woman with a look of fear in her eyes. "Take it," she said, and without a further word, ran past the four of us, the ghoul quick at her heels.

Charlotte and Mary acted at once, moving to the wooden door that the woman had been guarding. Charlotte beat it down with a few swift kicks and the two entered, leaving me behind with Machiavelli.

"Did you know that this would happen?" he asked, placing a hand gently on my shoulder.

"What, that I would be attacked and killed? Or well…you know," I said. I reached up and touched my throat, expecting to feel that sense of fear and impermanence that came with one of my false deaths. There was never confidence, never smugness, only fear. Except this time, the fear was lingering somewhere else. Instead, I felt nothing. "Like I said, it's happened before. Death accidentally removed my soul from my lifeforce when he was making me immortal the first time. Instead, he should have just severed my lifeforce while keeping my soul. He fixed that. This time, though, my lifeforce was already severed. I was already immortal—relatively speaking—when he unbound my soul. So, to answer your question, yes, I had a feeling that this would happen."

Machiavelli nodded and considered. He stared at the headless body of the ghoul, which was starting to dissolve in its own venomous drool. "I don't know if that makes you a reckless man or a foolish one."

"Does it matter?" I asked, cleaning my glasses on the only clean piece of cloth I could find on my tunic.

Machiavelli nodded. "Yes. Because if you are just reckless, then the consequences of your actions are never even considered. If you are foolish, then they are considered and then ignored."

That, surprisingly, made sense to me. "Well, either way, everything ended up alright."

"For you," he answered, then walked away to go and see what Charlotte and Mary had found. I stayed where I was, feeling those words hit me straight and true. They struck me sharply when most of the things I was feeling did not. When I had not even felt the fear my quasi-death brought me. I was soulless. I did not know what that meant, what was going to happen to me. I now knew, though, that I might not like the result.

The Medici vault—at least the one containing their mythical and magical items—was not at all what I expected. I suppose a part of me had been thinking that it would be like coming upon a dragon's hoard, with gold and jewels and things piled haphazardly around, gleaming like treasure ought to do. The reality was something rather different; it looked like someone had gone through and done a decluttering on a celebrity shoe collection. The items were placed neatly into little nooks that were carved into the stone walls. Each one held a tiny label and did not gleam at all.

It took Charlotte less than a minute to find the amulet. It, too, was not what I expected. Rather than some gold monstrosity like you would see in the movies, it was in reality little larger than a man's finger joint. The centre was a blue stone, like topaz or something, wrapped in a band of tarnished metal. It was cut in the shape of an eye and the tiny glyphs were a bit grimy, but other than that, there was hardly anything distinguishing about it.

Charlotte examined the amulet, then put the string over her neck and turned to Mary.

"Do you think she'll try to wield it?" a woman's voice purred in my ear. It was a familiar voice: seductive, tempting, invigorating. I turned to the owner and frowned.

"She's not that stupid," I said. I then realised who I was talking with and let out a yelp, leaping back slightly. "Life! What are you doing here?"

Everyone in the vault turned to look at our intruder. She clapped her hands giddily and fixed me with a grin that should have had me fairly melting on the floor from the intensity. All I felt instead was a mild tickle in the back of my mind. I frowned deeper. Life was dressed in what I would guess was the 1494 version of a cocktail dress. It was low-cut, purple with gold trim, probably more formfitting than it should have been given the modesty of women during the time period, and was about the only identifiable thing about her. The rest of her, as always, was ever changing. Impossible to pin down. I knew only that she was one of the most entrancing women I had ever encountered. This time, though, it was a little easier to look at her and to see past that horrible power that emanated from her. What I saw when I looked past that power was not good.

"Oh, crap," I said, leaping forwards to grab Machiavelli by the wrist and then pull him back. Mary was also drifting forwards. "Mary! Ah, crap. The Author!"

She shook her head, pressing her palm to her forehead. "What? Cal? What is going on?"

Charlotte, unsurprisingly, had drawn her sword and was pointing it at Life as though she were just any other intruder. I could see sweat beading on her brow and her breath was starting to turn ragged, though she had barely moved. I knew that effect. It was what Life did when people fought her, with will power or otherwise. She drew people in. She was the all-encompassing temptation. She was also wild, unpredictable, dangerous, and outright mean sometimes.

"Okay, okay, enough!" I shouted, forcing my voice louder than the power Life was emitting. I stepped between her and everyone else and jabbed her in the shoulder with a finger. "Tone it down a bit, alright?"

Life blinked, completely startled. The power dwindled until it was contained within her person, then she retreated into the open room with the dead ghoul. We followed her. Charlotte lowered her sword but did not sheath it. Machiavelli, having stood up so well against all the magical enemies we had just faced, not to mention his world being torn to pieces metaphorically speaking, was now trembling almost uncontrollably. Mary, too, looked a little ashen, though there was a touch of anger in her expression.

Life folded her arms and glared at me. "Who are you?" she demanded, drawing herself up. She was taller than me, but since I was just about as average height-wise as a person could get, that wasn't new. Not to mention I'd ignored her power before, even without having no soul. "Why can you touch me?"

"You mean without burning into a crisp while screaming my brains out?" I retorted. "Yeah, blame your husband for that."

Life looked closer at me, drawing near enough that I could feel her breath on my nose. Her eyes swirled, power focusing in the gaze. I imagine it would have been enough to burn me to pieces, had I been normal. Only problem was, I was far from normal and things weren't improving from there.

"You are human," Life said at last, pulling away. She sniffed. Folded her arms. "And you are immortal."

"Yes," I said.

"That is not fair. You should not be able to do that. I did not allow it." Life lifted her chin. Charlotte edged towards me, nudging me in the back and making me jump.

"This is Life?" she breathed in my ear. I nodded.

"Like I said," I continued, explaining to Life, "your husband did this to me. It's not my fault."

"My husband?" Life asked, her lips splitting into a grin that would have looked crazy on a madman. She took a step towards me. It was a sort of half-seductive dance that would definitely end up with me in serious trouble, except for the fact that I wasn't scared. I should have been. I really, really should have been, but I wasn't. Life stepped right up to me and brushed her hand down my cheek. "My husband isn't here."

"Oh, for crying out loud," I muttered, taking a self-preserving step back from Life. I tilted my head back and—trying to remember something that Yolanda had told me a while back when I discovered that Death didn't carry a cell phone and I couldn't just call him—summoned Death. "Chant thy name, thrice and done, Death, Dying and the Dead, beest thou a summoned one."

The room shattered into darkness around us. Life screamed, the sound pressing against my eardrums like a knife. I saw the others also press their hands to their ears. Charlotte's mouth was open in a scream. Mary and Machiavelli huddled together, the two least prepared to deal with the situation. I think they were too terrified to even scream. I just held on and endured.

After too long, Life stopped screaming. The darkness receded. Death stood calmly next to Life, brushing a stray piece of dirt off of his clothes. He looked around and saw the four of us huddled on the ground, covered in blood and dirt, the body of the ghoul nearly dissolved in the corner, Life standing there with a petulant look on her face. He coughed, bringing his impossibly black hand up to rub his neck nervously.

"Ah," he said. "Oops."

"Oops?!" Life snarled. Her power once again spread from her, flowing outwards and washing over everyone in the room until it collided with Death's power. Sparks crackled where the two behemoths touched.

"Ahem?" I asked, drawing the attention of the two powerful entities. They turned towards me and seemed to realise what they were doing. Death's power retreated swiftly, gracefully. Life's power lingered a moment before it, too, pulled back like a predator who had been disappointed at not catching its prey.

"What are you doing here, my dear?" Death asked. He reached out and ran a strand of Life's hair through his fingers. It looked like a black hole swallowing a star. Life clicked her tongue and tossed her head, pulling her hair free.

"I was coming to see if this warrior was going to be one of my champions," Life said, gesturing vaguely to Charlotte, still on the ground and catching her breath. "She has the Eye of Carteria. Who else would be brave enough to fight me?"

"Fight you?" Charlotte asked, voice a growl and her teeth ground together.

"No offence, lady," Mary said, struggling to sit up straight and leaning heavily on Machiavelli to do it. "But why would she fight you?"

"That's the only way to be a favoured of Life," I explained. "To seize Life and live to the fullest, you have to fight and struggle and do really stupid things."

"Dear," Life murmured, leaning towards Death while eyeing me uncertainly, "who is this human? He says that you made him immortal?"

"It is a very long story," Death replied, sounding a touch weary. I pinched the bridge of my nose between my fingers, trying to push back that annoyance that buzzed in my ear like a furious bee. Great, of all the emotions that remained for me to feel strongly, annoyance and anger had to be at the top of that list?

"It's really not that complicated," I said. "Time sent me back so that I could deal with the relationship problems between the two of you. Your husband from this time didn't realise that he had already made me immortal in the future and touched me. He—"

"You lost his soul?" Life widened her eyes and turned her full attention to her husband. He nodded, not in the least sheepish. Life, then, did something completely unexpected. This being her nature, I should very much have guessed that she would do something like this. Which would make the unexpected expected and gets into a whole lot of philosophy and mind-trickery that I don't have time for. Anyways.

Life squealed like a teenager at prom and flung herself at Death, wrapping her arms around him. Death chuckled, the sound rumbling, and wrapped his arms around her. Honestly, it was the most affectionate I had ever seen the two and it was a little startling. It was also a little graphic.

I coughed, pointedly, before they could start tearing clothes off of one another.

"That is amazing," Life said. She released Death from her embrace then ran over to me. It was like looking at a child running for a new and already-beloved toy. I held up my hand and she stopped mere inches from running into it.

"No. Ain't happening," I snapped. I lowered my hand and saw Life glaring at me again. I rounded on Death. "Seriously, this isn't helping at all! Do you have any idea what I'm supposed to do now? You got me into this mess—"

"And I did say that I would do my best to remedy my mistake," Death said, his normal solemn visage back in place. He stepped forwards until he stood beside Life. "But I tell you again, I do not know what it is that will bring my cousin here to return you to your normal time."

"I know precisely what to do," I said in a low voice. I turned to Charlotte and Machiavelli to help me out, but they stayed very far away from Life. Mary was still trembling. I saw Machiavelli try to look away and a slight green tinge touched his face. He was definitely feeling the effects of Life's presence. If I didn't want things to start going badly, I needed to get everyone away from here.

"You have said." Death inclined his head. He turned towards his wife and explained. "Cal claims that Time sent him back to mend the faults in out relationship before they begin, so that in the future we will not be quite so at odds."

Life snorted, then tossed back her head and laughed so that the sound echoed off the rock chamber. "Your cousin is a fool," Life told Death. She wiped a tear from an eye and continued to grin. "He understands nothing."

"Perhaps," Death said. He held out his hand for Life. "But still, I think we should leave them to their affairs. Have you finished with your champion?"

Life turned away from Death's hand and practically leaped towards Charlotte. The half-giantess drew her sword, taking several prudent steps back. Life clicked her tongue. "Tsk. I only wish to make my offer again. Are you so capricious as to turn me down? Do you care so little for Life?"

Charlotte shuffled her feet, getting into a deeper stance. "I care a whole lot for my life. You, on the other hand, are dangerous. You want me to *fight* you? Not going to happen."

Life shrugged, the motion careless. I narrowed my eyes. Life was not one to give up so easily. She hated being refused almost as much as she enjoyed the struggle that all the living endured to try and eke out an existence. "Very well," Life said, turning back to Death and sauntering towards him. "But know this, champion. I will be there when you try and wield that amulet. I will be there in every battle you face, in every decision you make to try and improve your lot. I am Life. If you wish to succeed, you will fight me. You may not know it, but you will."

Charlotte swung her sword through the air so that it made a very noisy slice. She pointed the tip at Life, brandishing the massive blade as though it were a butter knife. "I live on *my* terms. Not yours."

Life smiled languidly over her shoulder at Charlotte. Then, she sauntered back to her husband and kissed him noisily again. Before I could start complaining, she took Death's hand and in a flash, the two were gone. Sometimes I thought accepting Death's job offer was one of the dumbest things I had ever done. Most of the time, though, I just wanted to amend my contract.

I walked over to Charlotte and saw that she was worse off than I expected. Her face was pale and covered in a sheen of sweat. Her hands were shaking, barely able to keep the greatsword steady. She licked her lips nervously and looked at me. "Cal?" she asked, her voice low enough to prevent Mary and Machiavelli from hearing.

I shook my head. "I'm sorry," I said. "But she is not one to give up so easily. You may think you can beat her, but Life is wilful, capricious, unfair, dangerous, and wild. She can be marvellous, wonderful, beautiful. But she is never what you expect."

"And Death?" Charlotte asked in a hoarse whisper, lowering her sword. "Is he her opposite?"

"Death may seem steadier, but he is just as dangerous. He can be kind, yes, but he can be cruel. He doesn't care whether you're good or evil, whether you've accomplished everything or nothing. Everyone faces Death and no one wins."

"Except you." She looked at me with a dark expression, one I couldn't decipher. I hoped, desperately—enough so that I could feel it penetrate that barrier that kept everything shrouded in emptiness—that it wasn't fear. I took in a deep breath.

"I'm not sure losing my soul counts as winning," I said. I tried to smile, but the action felt forced. Once, when I had been at the top of my publicity and marketing game, smiling was second-nature. I felt every smile. I felt the confidence, the happiness. Now, I felt nothing. So I stopped smiling. I turned to find Mary whispering to Machiavelli. Both looked shaken, but generally whole.

"Shall we go?" Mary asked, letting Machiavelli's arm rest on her shoulder. I wasn't sure whether he was holding her up or she was supporting him. "I don't want to be down here when that vampire gets back with reinforcements. And I really don't want to explain why the essence of Life and Death is down here."

"Yeah," I said, holding out my hand to Charlotte. She straightened to her full height and ignored me, sheathing her sword and looking towards the exit. "Let's go."

"Agreed," Machiavelli said, falling into step behind Charlotte. Mary let me take her position then jogged to run up to Charlotte, putting her hand on the bigger woman's arm. "I have so many questions, for which I will demand answers, but that is for another time. This moment, I could sleep for a week."

I opened my mouth to agree and realised that I didn't feel tired. After having been up for nearly a whole day after a very brief rest and almost two days of no sleep, I should have been stumbling over my feet. I should have been starving. Desperate for water—or coffee. Instead, I felt nothing but a general weariness. An empty pit settled in the depths of my chest, perhaps the only manifestation of worry that this situation could allow.

The four of us marched back out of the Medici palazzo as though nothing had happened. We were all bloody, some of us injured, all of us ready to be away. This time, the servants were present, but they kept their heads low and their backs to the wall. I hoped that the rumours of this would be quelled by Alsatia or we were going to be hunted down by a whole lot of very dangerous beings. As we emerged into daylight, the city around us buzzed with movement and energy. The sun was almost at its peak. We must have been down in that dank basement for far longer than I realised.

"Cal and I are going back to my house," Machiavelli said. Mary turned and nodded.

"We'll meet up with you later. We need rest and then we'll figure out what to do next. This evening, for dinner at—crap. Charlotte! We have a problem!" Mary tugged on Charlotte's arm, looking like a teenager pulling at her mother's dress. Charlotte, looking wearier than even Machiavelli, shuffled to see what Mary was looking at.

"Well, crap," Charlotte said. She immediately held up her hands. Mary swallowed, then copied her. Machiavelli and I, slow on the uptake, did the same and then faced whatever was coming our direction. With that sort of reaction, I half expected a wild wyvern or something to be rampaging through the streets, headed straight for us. If Italy had wild wyverns. I wasn't quite sure about the magical beings native to the region. Instead, we were faced with something rather different.

A man wearing bright red robes that went down to to his calves, with a pair of white stockings or hose or whatever you called it, leather shoes in a maroon that went really badly with his robes, a heavy and thick golden necklace hanging down to the middle of his chest with an intricate cross on it, a cap on his head in that same garish red, and a look of supreme smugness, was leading a group of city guards. The guards looked like poorly dressed cousins compared to the swagger of this man. He stopped before us and I saw that the gaudy necklace-and-cross combination was not the only jewellery he wore; there were rings on three of his fingers, with one of them being one of those signet rings. The insignia looked important.

"Who're these guys?" I asked. Machiavelli made a sound in the back of his throat. Then, with a swift motion, he practically bowed at the waist to the man.

"Cardinal," he said, voice deep with respect. "I did not expect such an honour."

"And who are you?" the man asked. He waved away his question with a flick of his wrist. "Never mind. I have come to inform you that the respected Medici reported a theft from their personal vault this morning. Under Church and city law, you are to be placed under arrest. Guards."

"Ah," I said, nodding in understanding. "Not wyverns or goblins at all. Mortals. Indeed. Far more dangerous."

The guards surged forwards and arrested us. We were smart enough not to resist.

I didn't know a whole lot about the Church in 1494, but I had a feeling that they weren't responsible for arresting people. Or at least, they shouldn't have been throwing us into a dungeon. And, instead of some barracks type building below the street level, this was a true dungeon. The walls were covered in damp, moss was growing quite freely, the floors were stone and freezing cold despite the fact that it was a very pleasant spring day outside, and the smell was something dreadful that got up your nose.

Mary and Charlotte were interned somewhere else to keep the men and women separate. Machiavelli and I, though, were fortunate enough to be able to share a cell. We had been stripped of our weapons, and my belt purse was searched thoroughly, taking all of the earnings I had made from my brief stint as a city guard, and leaving my cell phone. And my glasses. They hadn't even seemed to notice that they were things that definitely did not belong in this time. I clutched my phone like a child's safety blanket.

We were then thrown into a small room with a single bucket in the corner, a solid wooden door with bars in the window, and not much else. I settled against the wall, leaning my head on a nice cushion of moss, prepared to wait. Machiavelli paced a bit, muttering to himself before he finally calmed down enough to also sit.

"This is wrong," he said. I raised my eyebrows and pushed my glasses up my nose. Machiavelli gestured with his hands, curling his fingers into fists. "This is beyond wrong. The Medici have influence with the Church, yes, but they should not control them like this. They should not be able to influence the Church into taking people prisoner and arresting them. We should be brought before the Signori, not thrown into a dungeon by the Church!"

"Don't get me wrong, but why is the Church arresting people? Shouldn't the city guard, the law people, be doing that?" I asked, my voice sounding oddly detached even to me. I was running my phone through my fingers, feeling its familiar weight and wondering just what my social media accounts were doing. I don't imagine that time spent in the far past was a useful excuse for not managing my clients' accounts. It occurred to me that I should have been more worried with the situation at hand, but I couldn't bring myself to care. I was a man out of time and I had long ago given up on trying to adjust to this horrible world of mine. Even my marketing skills, the very things that had gotten me into this mess, were completely useless. I might not have had a soul, but I still felt that loss keenly. More than keenly; I was pissed.

My entire life had been taken from me by Death. Okay, yes, I had been shot when Death first hired me, but there was no certainty that I would die. And, yes, not being dead was a whole lot better than being dead, but I was a human. Fragile, mortal, non-magical human. And Death threw me into a world of magic that I had hardly believed existed. I had been killed (sort of) multiple times, sent on impossible tasks, meant to deal with people who hated my very existence, all when I was hired to be doing nothing more than marketing and public relations. I was a marketer! I wasn't some hero to go about saving the world or repairing the relationship between Life and Death. I was jut Cal Thorpe and I wanted my life back. Death had stolen it from me and now he had gone and lost my soul. His wife was equally to blame for being reckless, cruel, enthralling and probably the source of all the problems between them.

Now here I was, stuck in a dungeon in 1494, a place where poor sanitation and plague was only a sneeze away. My allies were locked away. I had no access to the resources to which I was accustomed. And I couldn't even feel properly angry because my *soul* was missing.

Machiavelli sighed. He tilted his head back and

tightened his clothes around him as if to keep out of the cold which had already penetrated our bones. "Sometimes it is difficult to forget that you do not belong here. That you come from a world of magic and of beings that are nothing more than myth to many of us, blasphemy to the rest. Other times, it is hard to remember that you haven't always been here. To answer your question, the Church does not often take an active role in the prosecution of those who have broken the law, but on occasion, when there are special considerations that fall under Church provenance, the Church feels free to do whatever it wishes. It is a being of man, not of God. And it is men who are doing this to us now."

"Okay, so we fall under Church provenance, probably because of the magical connection," I said. That didn't really help us at all, as we were still stuck in what amounted to an underground prison. We had no weapons, we had no magic, and I highly doubted that the Church would take I'm from the future and I'm here to help as a valid reason for robbing the Medici, vampires or not. They would probably just burn me at the stake; I didn't really care to find out how that felt. "So how do we convince these men that we are not there enemies?"

Machiavelli let out a dry laugh, shaking his head. "You don't understand. The Church may not be considered kings, but they have the unequivocal rule of the people in this time. And when they choose to act, they are not often seen as wrong. They are very dangerous people to get on the wrong side of. And somehow, the Medici have convinced them that we are very dangerous people. You won't be able to just charm your way out of this. And we won't be able to fight our way out either."

"So what would you suggest we do?" I asked. Part of me had rather hoped that fighting our way out would be a valid option. The Church would learn that I couldn't be killed, would probably denounce me as demonic, and would probably try to exorcise me, but at least we would have *done* something. I realised though that that wasn't really a valid option. For me, perhaps, it would work. But I was not alone. Niccolo Machiavelli was interned here also, and he still had a role to play in history. If the church ostracised him, then he would be, to put it politely, snookered.

"I fear we are going to have to lie our way out," Machiavelli said. I turned to look at him, nearly dropping my phone in shock.

"I thought you said we couldn't charm our way out," I said. I pointed at him accusingly. "Lying is certainly part of that."

He shook his head, laughing dryly again, this time with a slight tinge of enjoyment in the gesture. "Charm implies faith in what you're saying. It implies that you are worth more than their time and they should just let you go. It implies that men find you likeable, trustworthy. I hate to break it to you, Cal, but that is not the case. You are bumbling. Endearing. Even capable. But I would not say that you are likeable or trustworthy."

"Gee, thanks," I said flatly. Truth was, I wasn't all that offended. Machiavelli had only known me barely a day before I had lost my soul, and things had gone rather downhill from there. I wasn't sure I even liked myself anymore, though I couldn't quite figure out if that was just a result of the lack of emotion or if it was something more.

Machiavelli held up a finger. "Lying, on the other hand, is spinning something into existence that does not require them to trust us, only believe us. It is conforming ourselves to their world view."

That was a little creepy, but then I considered the source. Some years from now he would be more than famous for writing a treatise in which he basically discussed the fact that the end justified the means and that manipulation was necessary. He was a political cynic and a person possessed of cunning and the ability to manipulate, to charm easily. Or he would be very shortly in the future. Based on those words, he was well on his way.

"I am all ears," I said, leaning my head back against the rock. "What would you suggest?"

"We simply have to discover what it is that these people, the Cardinal in particular, are afraid of."

"We could just tell him that the Medici offered us the amulet in exchange for killing someone," I suggested. Machiavelli winced, banging his head on the mossy wall behind him. He rubbed the spot and frowned.

"I doubt that would make them wish to release us," Machiavelli said. "No, we need to provide them with something that is so threatening that they feel it is safer to help us out into the world than it is to have us locked up. We need to find someone who is influential enough to cause problems should the Church be known to be holding us prisoner."

I considered, trying to remember all of the things that Machiavelli had told me and all of the things I remembered about this particular time in history. "What about the French?"

"The French?" Machiavelli asked, brows rising as he tried to process my answer. "Why would the French be threatening?"

"You said it yourself," I said. "You said the French were invading, and heading this direction. Surely that is a threat to the Church."

"The French king is known to be friendly towards the Church. Especially Rome. I doubt very much that they would care whether or not...Wait a minute. It is possible that...Do you remember what I said about Savonarola?"

"He is some sort of preacher?" I rubbed my forehead, feeling the start of a headache. It probably didn't help that I hadn't eaten or drunk anything since many hours earlier, and had since been killed once and argued with Life and Death. I didn't know what my physical limits were without a soul, but I was feeling a little tired. Not as tired as Machiavelli looked, but a little tired.

"Savonarola is a man who does not believe in the worldly possessions that the Medici, and by association, Florence, have acquired. He believes that the best way to grow close with God—as should be everyone's first objective—is to decry the wealth and temptations of this world. He believes that the Medici are corrupting people's souls and should therefore be stopped." Machiavelli looked at me as though I should understand the significance of this. All I saw was some religious figure who was against the Medici...

Against the Medici...

Who had used their influence with the Church to get us arrested...

"Is Savonarola favoured among the clergy here?" I asked. I started spinning my phone in my hand again, the familiar weight firing the synapses in my mind.

Machiavelli smiled. "The nobility, the landed gentry, did not find him particularly likeable, but he has a very large following amongst the populace. His influence is considerable."

I nodded, the plan forming in my mind too. "And if we were to inform them that we were under the protection of Savonarola...Would it work?"

"I have been to hear him talk. He is very charismatic. His words are perhaps honeyed, perhaps too formed for the masses, but he is extremely capable. That influence could very well be the means to our escape."

I nodded. This sounded like a very good plan. "Now we just need to tell the Church, that Cardinal in particular, no?"

"Yes," Machiavelli said. He stretched out his legs and crossed them at the ankles, straightening his tunic thing and brushing off some dirt. I rose to my feet, prepared to shout for guards and demand an audience with the Cardinal. I looked at Machiavelli in confusion. He folded his fingers together, looking for all the world like he had no intention of doing anything other than taking a nap.

"Aren't we going to go talk to the Cardinal?" I asked, waving at the iron bars keeping us imprisoned. Machiavelli shrugged.

"I have a feeling that they will not come and talk with us for a very long time. The Church is not a fast moving creature. I would suggest you get comfortable. We might be here a while."

With that, I sighed in disgust and sank back down to the floor. "Do you know, I'm beginning to really hate your time."

"Ah, yes, but we have good wine," Machiavelli pointed out. I narrowed my eyes and clutched my phone tighter. "'Tis a pity there is none to be found at the moment. That would make the waiting more bearable."

"None of the books I've read about you said you had a sense of humour," I grumbled.

"And now that you know the truth?"

"I would say they're pretty accurate."

Machiavelli snorted and shook his head. "You are a strange man, Cal. I find that I am pleased to have gotten to know you."

"Even though I introduced you to a world of magic and terror?" I asked, somehow actually curious. Machiavelli considered. I saw lines form at the corner of his eyes and his mouth twitched into a frown. He looked at me, finally focusing on the phone in my hand. Machiavelli swallowed, closed his eyes, and said nothing.

Fair enough.

WE HAD BEEN SITTING in that cell for several hours, each of us taking the time to doze as best we could. It was not terribly comfortable, but the moss at least provided some cushion against the stone. But after a while, Machiavelli and I just sat there, waiting for something interesting to happen. He figured that they would have to bring us food at some point, but I wasn't quite so certain. After all, I had read stories about the Church and their treatment of people. It wasn't always pretty.

"Describe again to me this…sand-ish," Machiavelli said. I sighed and shook my head, probably getting moss in my hair but not really caring.

"It's a sand*wich*, okay? Named after the Earl of Sandwich. He was the one who lay claim to Hawai'i and you have no idea what I'm talking about. Anyways, you take two slices of bread. You put mustard, mayonnaise, whatever, on the bread. Then lettuce. Tomato. Onion. Meat. Cheese. Then you put everything together in one great stack and eat it."

"It sounds complicated."

"A sandwich sounds complicated? Geez, wait until I try to explain a pressure cooker!" I said. Machiavelli looked like he was going to ask—and considering we had nothing else to do, I would have attempted to answer despite the fact that I really didn't understand how the technology worked—when I heard something. I held out my hand, signalling for him to stop talking. He closed his mouth, looking about.

"What is that?" he whispered. I shook my head; I didn't know.

It sounded like a hiss, coming at us from many different directions at once. The sound grew louder and I could finally identify the source. It was coming from a drain set in one of the corners, too small for any human to climb through. Something was in there, and it was coming straight for us.

I looked around for a weapon of any sort and came up with nothing. So I stood and walked over to the drain, waiting for whatever was coming through to emerge so I could squish it. Or, at least, determine if I needed to—or would be able to—squish it. What came out gave me pause, enough so that it had lunged at me and sank its teeth into my leg before I could do anything.

I shook the creature from my leg, throwing it into the corner. It didn't seem at all fazed, gathering itself and letting out a hiss twice as loud as before. Machiavelli whispered in my ear, making me jump, "What *is* that?"

"I have no idea."

The thing looked like a tiny dragon-wyvern thing. It had a long neck, four legs tipped with needle-sharp claws, a tail only slightly longer than its neck. It was obviously a dragon. Except that it had the face of a cat. A very angry, very intelligent cat. At our words, the creature huffed and sat back on its hind legs, its tail twitching in an extremely cat-like manner.

"I am a Tatzelwurm, you ignorant humans!" the creature said. I covered my mouth with my hand, holding back a snort of laughter. Machiavelli failed in his own attempt, chuckling audibly. The creature straightened its neck, visibly affronted. "Why do you laugh?!"

"We're sorry," I said behind the smile. "But... you sound like a tiny kitten!"

The Tatzelwurm arched its back and hissed, spreading foul breath and probably-poisonous venom. Machiavelli crawled backwards, holding an arm over his mouth. I just waved away the fog and the venom. "Wrong move, buddy," I grumbled. "I've had a bad day."

The Tatzelwurm screeched, its ears flat against its head. It lunged for me just as I lunged for it. All my experience with magical creatures in the last year hadn't taught me as much as it should have, but I was quite good at putting my hands on slippery creatures like the Tatzelwurm. Its head slipped past me enough that it was able to sink its fangs into my shoulder. But that left me free to wrap a hand around the base of its head and the middle of its stomach. With a wrench, I pulled the creature from my shoulder, leaving two gashes that I probably should have felt more than I did.

"No!" the thing yowled, wriggling as best it could. I held it at arms' length and the tiny legs of this cat-dragon-wyvern-thing couldn't manage to scratch me. It was completely useless. "Unhand me, cretin!"

"Not until you tell me how you managed to find us in here," I said.

"Cal," Machiavelli said in a warning tone. "Perhaps you should let the poor creature go."

That, as it turns out, was the wrong thing to say. The Tatzelwurm started wriggling even more than it had done. Its scaled skin slipped through my hands until it managed to catch a claw in my sleeve. I pulled away, the Tatzelwurm pulled away and both of us ended up stuck. The Tatzelwurm tugged on the snagged claw, but was firmly fixed in my sleeve. A moment later and it started making the strangest noise.

It took me a few seconds to realise that the creature was crying. "J-just let me go!" it mewled.

"Answer my question and I'll let you go," I said. The thing pulled helplessly at its snagged claw, but the good craftsmanship of 1494 cloth held firm. It wasn't going anywhere. The Tatzelwurm stopped struggling and nodded.

"You have bested me," it hiccoughed. "You…may have a boon."

"Alrighty, then," I said. I let go both of my hands, the Tatzelwurm fell through the air, but it managed to un-snag its claw and landed, as all cats do, on its feet. The thing hissed and edged towards the tiny drainage hole.

"Oh, no you don't," I said, stepping over the hole. The wurm slunk backwards towards Machiavelli. To my surprise, the future political genius reached out and touched the Tatzelwurm behind its ears. It squeaked, but Machiavelli's fingers scratched it gently. The creature seemed to relax almost immediately. Even Machiavelli seemed calm.

I gaped.

"We had many cats on my father's estate," Machiavelli explained.

"I am not a cat," the Tatzelwurm complained, though it leaned into Machiavelli's touch. "I am a Tatzelwurm!"

"And how did you find us, Tatzelwurm," I asked, trying to sound calm. I even put on a smile, though this one, like many others recently, felt off. My normal good cheer and affability were waning. I hoped it was just to do with being trapped in a dungeon in Renaissance Italy.

The Tatzelwurm sniffed, just as I've seen cats do a hundred times. "I heard you through the drains. It was easy enough to climb up and find you. You are far more entertaining than the other two. They just keep complaining at the loss of a sword or something."

"The other two," Machiavelli breathed, his fingers pausing in their ministrations. The Tatzelwurm shook itself, scales rustling, then stepped a few paces away, licking its claw. "Charlotte and Mary."

I nodded. It wasn't entirely surprising that they should be trapped down here, too, but I had half thought that they would be taken somewhere else, being that they were women. I turned to the Tatzelwurm and pointed my phone at it. It blinked. "I need you to go find those two and deliver a message."

"Why would I do that? I have already answered your question. I have half a mind to just go find entertainment elsewhere," the creature said loftily. "You are not even suitable eating."

"What *would* you consider suitable eating?" I asked, having an idea. This creature was part cat, yes, but it was also part dragon-wyvern-thing. And their appetites were notorious. Even mentioning food had this creature's tongue darting out to lick its muzzle. It disguised the action a moment later by giving its face a thorough bath.

"You cannot tempt me by such means."

"Lamb? Cream? Fish?" I asked, trying to think of the sorts of food a cat would like. At the last, I saw the Tatzelwurm's eyes widen. It gave its scales a shake, winding its sinuous body towards me.

"Perhaps we can come to some sort of arrangement after all," it said. It looked between Machiavelli and myself. "I would require payment from the both of you."

"As you like, Tatzelwurm," Machiavelli agreed. "But we really must pass a message on to our friends."

"Agreed," I said. "You will have your fish."

The Tatzelwurm nodded and extended its tail to me. I took it and shook it gently, watching as it repeated the process with Machiavelli. Then, it sat back and curled its tail several times around its claws. "Very well, speak your message."

I looked at Machiavelli and he explained in a few succinct phrases about Savonarola and our plan to use the unsuspecting friar to win our freedom. If the guards came to Charlotte and Mary first, they were to say a few key things and then loudly declare themselves devoted assistants of Savonarola. After all, why else would the Medici have us imprisoned? If the guards came to us first, we would do the same thing and then come fetch them. The Tatzelwurm nodded, showed us its fangs in a yawn, and lunged past me to dive into the drain and disappear into the dark. I stumbled backwards, nearly dropping my phone.

"Geez, a little warning would have been nice," I said, frowning. I wiped my phone on my tunic and sighed at the resulting smudge.

"It was a cat," Machiavelli pointed out. "They are not often in the habit of providing warnings. What is that thing you keep playing with?"

I sat back down beside Machiavelli and turned my phone on. "It's a means of communication and, uh, stuff. We can capture pictures, talk to people all over the world by voice or by text or by seeing their face. And there's the internet."

The screen lit up, causing Machiavelli to jump. I glanced at the battery: 50%. Not bad, actually, considering I'd been stuck in pre-electricity Italy for a couple of days, now. Granted, it had been off for much of that time, but still. Machiavelli reached out to touch the screen, poking at the internet browser button. It activated and Machiavelli jumped further.

I took a selfie of Machiavelli and myself, showing him the resulting image. His eyes widened and I thought he was about to pass out. "This is *astonishing*! To have such a realistic representation, without having to sit for a painter. It is as though you and I exist in this tiny machine. I...This is impossible."

"Not impossible," I said, "just very cool."

He coughed uncomfortably and moved an inch away. "Tell me about this internet."

"Well, it's sort of like…a library. It has all of this information about history, about finances, about current events. People put their lives on the internet and sometimes they become famous. That's my specialty, making sure people are seen. And the thing that you opened, Google, is like the ability to search for whatever information you want and finding it in an instant."

Machiavelli nodded, obviously still not terribly keen on this whole concept. He pointed at the screen. "Can you search for what appointment Death is meant to miss?" he asked. I started to shake my head and say that it didn't work like that when I considered. Maybe Death's appointments were on the internet.

"I don't know," I said, but my thumbs were already flying. I searched for Death, appointment and 1494, hit enter, and only then realised that I shouldn't be able to do such a thing. I shouldn't be able to have access to Google at all, yet there I was, searching away. And the thing was loading, too.

I had access to the internet.

This changed *everything*.

The search results popped up a moment later. A bunch of it was to do with the Medici—been there, done that—and some still to do with the Black Death, not a pleasant time. But then I found a mention of several poets and authors and writers who had said that they (or their characters) had an appointment with Death.

Death's appointment wasn't with Life. It was with a person. His missed appointment was with a person who was supposed to die.

I hunched over my phone, typing furiously away and hoping that that internet didn't vanish a moment later. I spent perhaps five minutes digging through records of Florence in 1494, looking for deaths. And then, I found one.

"Have you heard of a Giovanni Abrami?" I asked, looking up from my phone. I pushed my glassed up my nose and saw Machiavelli's confusion plain as day.

"No," he said. "But that does not necessarily mean anything. I am still fairly new to the city and have not made as many connections as many years here would bring. Is he important?"

I shook my head. "I don't think so. Apparently, he's a mildly capable fur merchant who succumbs to the Black Death and leaves some money to the Church. Google barely thought him worth a mention, but he's the only person who makes sense. Mildly important, enough so that perhaps he would be difficult if he remained alive."

Machiavelli brushed off the front of his long tunic, nodding. "Very well then. We shall go find this Giovanni Abrami and make certain that Death finds him also."

I held up my phone with a cry of triumph, which is exactly how the guards found us a moment later. Charlotte and Mary were standing behind the slightly-cowed guards, looking not the least bit surprised at our predicament. Charlotte had her sword back and Mary was scribbling at her scroll, glaring at the guard.

"I take it you have a plan," Charlotte said while the guards unlocked us. "One that does not involve that strange creature you sent our direction?"

"Oh, yes," I said, feeling a little bit more like my normal self. "I have a plan."

TIME'S UP

Machiavelli insisted that we stop by his house before we went running off after this Abrami fellow so that we could change clothes and get something to eat. I wasn't feeling particularly hungry, but the other three were flagging. And we were all wearing clothes with varying amounts of blood on them. My own were the worst, but as my long over-tunic was black, it was harder to see. Still, it was a prodigious amount of blood.

Charlotte and Mary sank happily into the chairs at Machiavelli's table. I went up the stairs to the tiny bedroom that had been mine for the last day and washed my face and neck while Machiavelli fetched some other clothes for me. Unfortunately for me, the hose and codpiece were still relatively clean. All I had to change was my undershirt, doublet (another contraption that hit me mid thigh and this time in a horrid green), and long tunic thing. I grumbled the entire time I was putting them on, knowing full well that I was getting all the names wrong and driving Machiavelli crazy.

If I was right, though—and I was right—then I would soon be rid of this terrible clothing and back to my own home where I could lounge about in sweats and a t-shirt for at least a month, bingeing on television shows and popcorn. A perfectly normal existence. Death and Time and Life and everybody else would just have to leave me be for a while. I could even go out to the mortal realms and wander around like a normal person.

Pure bliss.

The imaginings faded away as Machiavelli led the way back down the stairs. Charlotte and Mary had put a sizeable dent into one of the dead birds I had seen the day before, now cooked. I took a few pieces and some bread, putting them together in a makeshift sandwich before moving to the door. "Come on, gang, we've got things to be doing!" I said.

"Cal, cannot you wait for a few minutes?" Machiavelli grumbled, but he was already copying my sandwich and striding towards the door. Charlotte and Mary were only a few steps behind him.

"I don't imagine that we'll have a whole lot of time," I said. "After all, why else would I have been dropped in the here and now? No, we have to go do this as quickly as possible."

"You propose walking into the house of a plague victim to be certain that he expires," Machiavelli said. Mary halted, bringing out little group to a stop.

"Wait, this guy is supposed to be a plague victim?

Oh, no. There's no way I'm going anywhere near him." Mary shoved her charcoal into her belt purse and folded her arms, looking for all the world like an impetuous teenager about to put her foot down.

"You will come," Charlotte said, her voice brooking no argument. "We are fulfilling our side of the bargain with Cal. However, if you so wish, you can remain outside and keep watch."

"Keep watch for what, plague doctors?" Mary snapped.

"Death, or Life," I said. Mary's expression twisted into a scowl; obviously that was not a much better option. "Alright, Niccolo, where are we going?"

Machiavelli took a breath, as if he, too, were about to argue about this plan, then shook his head. He turned and started walking along the cobbled streets of Florence. We followed behind him, passing squares and courtyards. We passed near the wealthy section of the Medici and their like, then turned down a different street.

"Many of the merchants live in this area," Machiavelli explained. "Though I do not know if Giovanni Abrami is among them. Surely, though, someone will know of his whereabouts."

"And what are we going to do once we find him?" Mary grumbled. "Kill him if he's not already dead?"

"That would be one way to make sure the appointment stays on track," I said, blinking a little at the obvious cheer in my voice. Was that from the prospect of returning home or from preparing to kill a man. I wasn't certain.

Charlotte paused and narrowed her eyes at me. "Cal, are you certain of this plan? There seems to be a great deal that is left to chance. We do not even know for certain that this man is meant to be Death's appointment."

"It's him, alright!" I snapped. "And there's nothing wrong with my plan. This is the best way to make sure that I do what I was sent here to do. I helped you get your Eye thing, didn't I?"

Charlotte took a deep breath through her nose. Mary folded her arms and glared at me. But the half-giantess nodded and released her breath. "Yes, you did. And as I have said, we will help you fulfil your end of the bargain. I just…question the prudence of this plan. There seems to be little evidence of—"

"Look, I know that there's not a lot of evidence," I said. I waved my phone at Charlotte. "But I have the internet, and it's telling me that Giovanni Abrami is someone who would be potentially problematic if he were to remain alive. There is no one else. So we're going to go in there and we're going to make sure that he meets Death."

My three companions exchanged a look. Machiavelli sighed and shook his head, but said nothing. Charlotte, too, remained quiet, her expression hard. Mary had none of the qualms of the others; she asked the question that seemed to be on everyone's mind. "And you're just going to kill the man?"

Maybe if I still had my soul, I would have hesitated. I would have considered the cost of killing a man. Potentially an innocent man, but still one who had to die. As it was, my lack of emotions said nothing about the ethical dilemma. I just weighed the options, and nodded. Firmly. "If it's the only way, then yes."

"That's what I was afraid of," Mary said. She turned on her heel and marched onwards. Charlotte moved after her, throwing me a frown over her shoulder. Machiavelli put a hand on my shoulder.

"It is good that you have us with you. I am not certain that you should be doing this alone," he said. Whatever that meant.

"Let's just get this over with, okay?" I grumbled, hunching my shoulders. He nodded and moved off after Mary and Charlotte, exchanging a few words with them before taking the lead. After a while, Machiavelli stopped in a square to ask directions. I stopped paying attention to the splendour of the city, the statues, the art, the carvings, the greenery. I just wanted to find this Abrami and get back to my normal time. We were pointed to a section of the city farther inwards. A few twists and turns and then we were there.

Only…something wasn't right.

The house upon which we looked had been closed off, presumably to keep people away from a victim of the plague. I didn't know a whole lot about the quarantine practises of the time, but I imagine the windows being boarded up and the upper ones being covered with black cloth weren't a good sign. However, the people carrying a stretcher with a body was the current problem. They wore the heavy black robes that I had come to expect from the modern idea of the plague doctors; there was even that funny mask that looked like a bird beak. But if this was the right house—and I trusted Machiavelli's guidance on that—then the body being carried out was that of Giovanni Abrami. And if Giovanni Abrami's body was being carried out, then he was dead. Death had kept his appointment here.

We had the wrong person.

And I had no idea who else it could possibly be.

"This isn't right," I said, taking a frantic step forwards. Charlotte held out an arm to hold me back, more than strong enough to keep me contained. "No, he's not supposed to be dead! We were supposed to remind Death of his appointment and then he was supposed to die. He has to be the missed appointment!"

"He is not," Charlotte said, her eyes hard and her mouth pulled into a tight line. "We must look elsewhere."

"You don't understand." I pulled my phone out of my belt purse and showed it to her. "There *is* no one else. There is *nothing* else that makes sense."

"Then we have failed." The words fell to the stones at my feet, plain as day. I felt the last few days catch up to me. Even the absence of my soul could not manage to keep away this sudden weariness, this horrible sense of loss. I swayed on my feet, looking between my three companions and the body of Giovanni Abrami, being carried far away.

"Come," Machiavelli said, clapping me on the shoulder. He looked about as pleased as I felt, which was to say, not very. "I believe it is time for a drink."

BETWEEN CHARLOTTE, Mary, Machiavelli and I, we scrounged up enough money to wallow in self-pity for a good long while. We camped out at a table practically covered in bottles and jugs of wine, the only break a platter of breads and meats and cheeses with some grapes. My mortal companions dove for the food before drowning themselves in wine. I, on the other hand, lingered over another makeshift sandwich, alternating bites with sips of wine. I would never get drunk this way, but I was unlikely to feel the effects of the wine anyways.

Just another lovely byproduct of having no soul.

"I should never have shaken his hand," I said, laying my head on my arms. "All of this would be a distant dream but for that."

"What are you talking about?" Mary asked, dropping a hand on my shoulder. I shifted enough to be able to look up at the journalist and sighed.

"Death," I said, sounding far more morose than I intended. Machiavelli snorted into his third glass of wine. I guess he was moving towards that lighthearted buzzed drunk feeling. Good for him. I propped my head in my hand. "About a year ago, I was walking to a dinner through the park and got shot. Ah, um, a fast moving projectile object—"

"We are familiar with guns," Machiavelli said, an amused gleam in his eye. "We have had cannons and even smaller guns for nearly a century, now."

"Right," I groused. "Apparently I need to read more. Anyways, I got shot. And then Death appeared, offering me a job. He said that he could only have appeared to me in the Instant of Death, in his realm. But he also said that there was a slight chance I could survive, or something along those lines. I was too stupid, though. I decided that adventure and immortality were much better than potentially dying and living in a whole lot of pain. If I hadn't been so stupid, then I wouldn't be caught up in this mess. I wouldn't have been thrown into a world of magic, where everything is as dangerous as you could possibly imagine, where half of the world wants to kill me, where my own *boss* is like the biggest nightmare people have, and I wouldn't have been sent back in time to this…this…technological backwater!"

There was a beat after my rant. Charlotte clapped at my frustrations, her expression flat. Mary, though, burst out laughing. "You would give up all of *this* for being normal?!" she chuckled, wiping moisture from her eyes. "What an idiot!"

I straightened and downed the rest of my glass of wine. Feeling a proper rush of anger, I jabbed a finger in Mary's direction. "You think that chasing after that adrenaline rush, that addiction, is so good? What happens when you end up in a terrible situation, one of your own making, and you can't get out of it? Or worse, what happens when the adrenaline no longer gets your heart pumping? This world is messed up, no question. All I want is my quiet little corner of it, that keeps me from going insane, alright? I don't need dragons or rock trolls or air spirits or giants or *anything*! I'm a PR agent, okay? I know when a ship is sinking, when there's too much craziness for people to handle. And this ship, it's sinking. You know why? Because we're up against Life and Death, two entities that could level the entire planet, let alone you or me. So, yeah, I would happily give all of this up if I could return to normal. It was a mistake, trusting Death. All it's brought me is failure."

Another beat of silence. Mary slumped back in her seat, glaring at me, but she thankfully said nothing. Charlotte's flat expression shifted as she quirked a single brow, but she took a sip of wine and, too, said nothing. Only Machiavelli bothered to speak and I should have known that his words would be the worst of the three.

"It seems to me, Cal, that you are pining for something that will never come to pass. We cannot go backwards. You are, whether you like it or not, an employee of Death. And you are, like it or not, here in this time and this place. It is your own fault if you do not see the boon in that. You would give up wonder for ignorance. Perhaps you need to rethink your priorities." He looked at me over the rim of his cup, then shook his head. "This is not my world, either, Cal. Or have you forgotten?"

I sighed, perhaps melodramatically, but it was enough to clear my mind just a touch. "Look, I appreciate everything that you all have done for me. But the fact of the matter is, I just want all of this to be over so I can go home. Is that so wrong?"

Machiavelli studied the wine in his cup. Mary rooted around in her bag for some charcoal, though she didn't actually pull any out. Charlotte, though, sighed and shook her head. "I once thought as you did. It is not easy being a half-giantess thrown into the world with no defences. I had just enough connection to the magical world to travel and find the artefacts, but my resources in the human world were limited. Yet here I am, having successfully retrieved the Eye of Carteria."

"With help," I pointed out. Charlotte shrugged.

"I would not have it any other way. You must come to terms with your place in this new world. You must stop thinking of the danger and of your own failure. Everyone fails, Cal. That's what Life is about. Failing. And then learning and moving on. So what if you misdiagnosed the appointment that Death is meant to keep? There were two parts to your task, were there not?"

"Yeah." I pushed away my plate of food and looked longingly at the wine. I wanted to drown my sorrows in drink. It was never really my thing, truth be told, but now that the option was taken from me, I longed for it. Instead, I forced myself to sit up and felt my bones creaking as I did. Maybe I was more tired than I thought. Perhaps I shouldn't push my limits with my lack of soul. Perhaps I should take it easy…well, easier, at least. After this pity party, I decided I was going to go take a nap.

"Life was to, what, refuse Death something?" Charlotte prompted.

I perched my glasses on top of my head and rubbed the heels of my palms into my eyes. "Yeah. Um, Life was going to refuse Death a mortal who was meant to die. I've never heard of that happening. I mean, she gets pissed at him for taking people, but she hasn't ever stopped him that I know of. It's not like a person can avoid Death, right? Besides, he doesn't actively kill them, he just…you know. Anyways, I wouldn't even know how to go about figuring out who—"

I was cut off by a scream, high pitched and terrified. In my experience, that usually meant something was going really, really wrong.

As one, the four of us abandoned our drinking binge and ran outside to see what was going on. What faced us was, in a word, bad.

The centre of the square, which had previously been a nicely tended little garden around which people could sit while talking or resting, was now nothing but rubble. The plants had withered and died and been strewn with rocks pulled from the wall surrounding the garden and the cobbled streets. The pedestrians and lookie-loos were backing away from the scene of destruction, but the two figures facing off across the square prevented them from going too very far.

Life and Death were standing there in all their glory and power, glowering at one another. Given the screams from the people now trapped, I had a feeling that everybody could see them. And that was really not good.

"You cannot," Death snapped, his dark power slithering forwards, insidious and terrible. Life tossed her head back and laughed, brushing his power away with a flash of her own tempting and overwhelming power.

"Why not?" Life demanded. She spotted me and

pointed accusingly in my direction. "You have this one, do you not? You have bent *all* the rules!"

"That was an accident," Death said, holding up his hands. He took a step towards Life and was rebuffed. He glared at me instead. "I am working to remedy it."

Life guffawed, the sound sweet and piercing. I saw Machiavelli sway, eyes closed as he tried to shake off the desperate need to go to Life. I had experienced that sensation before; it was not easy to resist her. Even as we stood there, a woman with a basket of fruit on her arm stumbled towards Life, reaching out to touch her, eyes wide and beseeching. Life brushed her away with an impatient flick of her hand. The touch of her skin was quite deadly, though, and the woman let out a shrill scream as a ghostly fire consumed her.

Charlotte stepped forwards, teeth bared in a snarl. "No!" she said, drawing that ridiculous sword.

Life turned her head to stare at Charlotte. I would have sworn that I saw a flicker of lust in Life's eyes, but it was impossible to pin her true emotions down. "Yes," Life hissed, sidling towards the four of us. "Fight me, champion. Fight me and take your place!"

"You cannot have her," Death said, moving towards us as well. He stretched out his hand and sent a rippling dark wave towards us. Mary squeaked and shuffled backwards. Charlotte caught her, waved her hands furiously while angry-whispering, and shoved her into the tavern. She cast a hard glance at Machiavelli.

"You can either help us or join her. I would suggest you join her," Charlotte said, voice firm. Machiavelli looked at the two titans standing in the square, glaring at each other and moving closer and nodded before, he, too, vanished inside the tavern.

Charlotte looked at me and raised her brows. I swallowed, nodded, and strode into the square. "What the heck is going on here?!" I demanded.

"Get out of the way," Life snarled. "You have interfered too much already!"

Before I could even think of a response, Life waved her hand and I was quickly assaulted by her power. It was sharp and poignant, filling my lungs as I took in a breath and making everything seem far less interesting. Life filled me with energy; I was eager and interested and nothing could stop me. All I had to do was enjoy everything that came my way. There was no need to fret about lost technology or people left behind. So what if my normal life had been dropped by the wayside? I had adventure and intrigue and wonder right within my grasp. Who *wouldn't* want to live as I did? I just needed to embrace it. Embrace my life. Embrace Life.

"—Cal!" Charlotte slammed into me, knocking me to my knees. I looked around and saw that Life was staring at Death with wild, uncontainable fury in her eyes. He returned the look with coldness and emptiness and utter, soul-deep calm. He would not be ruffled by her tantrums. He was Death.

"I thought you were immune," Charlotte hissed in my ear, helping me to stand. I shook my head.

"I can shake it off, and I won't die if either one of them touches me, but I'm far from immune. I haven't been hit by that sort of power for a while. It hurts," I said. I pressed my hand to my head. The people still in the square stared at Charlotte and I as though we had just experienced some sort of horror. Death and Life ignored us, preferring to face each other.

"We have to stop them," Charlotte said.

"Or they'll level Florence," I agreed. I stood fully straight and nodded. "Alright. Come on, let's go do some serious relationship counselling."

Charlotte gave me a strange look, but said nothing. That was probably a good thing. My poor sense of humour was at best a half-step away from hysteria. The only thing preventing me from screaming or giggling was the fact that my soul was very, very far away and I couldn't feel things as I usually did.

"Death!" I yelled, projecting my voice as best I could. Death spared me half-a-glance, which was still strong enough to make me queasy. "Enough!"

"Be quiet, tiny human," Death said in a voice that echoed through the air like inevitability. Life chuckled darkly.

"Why don't you listen to your plaything, husband dear?" Life sneered. She danced forwards and snatched at me, laughing as I jerked away. "Oh, scared are you?"

"You bet your left eye I am," I said, taking a few more precautionary steps away. Charlotte had vanished into my peripheral vision; I hoped she was doing something clever and preparing an ambush or something. "What is *wrong* with you people?" I said.

Life snorted and shook her head. She backhanded me before I could do anything but blink and I crashed into the remains of the garden. The plants around me withered further as Death's power surged forwards. I felt the air around me tighten, the light darken. I was still able to breathe and move easily, but I saw some of the people around turning grey, their eyes wide as they struggled for life.

"You would *dare*," Death breathed at his wife. "Your antics have gone one step too far, this time."

"My *antics*?!" Life laughed, the sound brittle. She ramped up her own power to meet Death's halfway into the square and they mingled together, too overwhelming for anything—plant or stone—that stood in their path. Life's already everchanging appearance became harder to bear. Her beauty, her tantalising nature, even her scent, seemed to overpower my other senses so that all the world except for Life fell away. "My *antics* are what my nature entails! I am meant to be enjoying all of the things the world has to offer. Dancing. Partying. Battles. Arguments. Passion. It's *mine* and you can't have it!"

"All things come to an end, wife, dear," Death said, his own voice still deeply calm and cold. At the words, my breath fogged and my temperature dropped. I staggered to my feet, knowing that if I didn't do something, this day's destruction would only bring about a whole lot more in the future. I had to stop them now before they truly went to war. "And that is *my* domain. You have no place there."

"Thief! You take *everything* that I love!" Life screamed, hands clenched into fists at her sides.

"Petulant child," Death countered. He curled his lip

in a look of contempt and I knew that things were about to get a whole lot worse. Death surged forwards, moving towards Life as if nothing stood in his way. Only, someone did.

A child, a young girl, stood frozen as the two forced converged on her. She had been trying to run for the tavern and safety and instead was standing directly between Life and Death. Charlotte was staring, wide-eyed, at the girl. Her sword was out and her feet were moving, but the combined powers of Life and Death were mixing together and affecting even her; she was too slow.

I lunged forwards, shoving away any lethargy, any pain that lingered. I could feel the blood dripping down my neck from where my head had hit some of the rubble, but that didn't matter. Nothing mattered except the fact that the two most powerful beings I had ever seen were going to converge in an attack right at the spot where an innocent child stood. I forced myself to move faster.

My arms wrapped around the girl, too slow to push her away. All that I could do was flatten her beneath me, shielding her with my body, as Death and Life converged above me. There was a sound, like a thousand people screaming in horror or ecstasy. I couldn't tell you which it was. Pain, worse than even I had felt when my soul was severed, flared through me. This time, the world didn't turn white, it turned red. I opened my mouth to howl, but no sound came out. Probably because my mouth was gone. *I* was gone.

And then I wasn't.

My body reformed, pulling itself back together from the depths of whatever oblivion I could never reach. My arms, my chest, my fingers, all of it came back together from a million pieces. Somewhere in my reforming, my mouth and throat returned so that I could scream. I threw my head back and shrieked to the sky, certain that this was my end. Only, it wasn't.

I don't know how long it took for me to piece myself together again, only that I was covered in sweat and blood by the time I was done. I panted heavily, all my muscles trembling. But—a miracle—the girl that I had shielded looked up at me, alive. She was a bit scraped from where I had tackled her to the ground, but she was alive and well.

I pushed myself off of her, sitting up. My clothes had been obliterated, but I didn't really care about dignity. I forced my muscles to cooperate as I looked between Life and Death. They were both still, gaze fixed on me. Death could not seem to form words, though his jaw worked up and down. Life recovered first.

"Very well," she said, pointing at Death. "You want my champion? You think you can keep your 'appointment' with her? Then you have to go through me to do it!"

Life moved, faster than the eye could follow. She appeared beside Charlotte who was breathing heavily from the residual power in the air. Charlotte's sword lifted, the point tracing Life, but she was too fast, too powerful. Life wrapped her hand around Charlotte's arm. "She is *mine*," Life said.

Charlotte screamed, the touch of Life burning her even through her leather armour and clothes. Life tilted back her head and roared with laughter. A light filled the square, forcing me to close my eyes. When I looked back, Life was gone. So was Charlotte.

"You should not have done that, Cal," Death said lowly. He was as close to angry as I have ever seen. "She was not meant to escape me."

Then, in an absence of light that was as equally blinding as Life's departure, Death, too, vanished.

The square fell silent. The people trapped there by Life and Death's altercation seemed to hold their breath for a minute. Then, as if air had been sucked back into the world, activity broke out. People fled the scene. The little girl that I had shielded from Death ran to her mother across the square. There were few injuries that I saw; one man had a scrape on his head from where some of the cobbled stones had thrown themselves towards him. Another woman looked dirty and harried, but unhurt but for a twisted ankle. These impressions lasted only a few seconds, though, because the square emptied almost faster than I could blink. Then, I was alone.

"Where is she?"

Okay, not alone.

I twisted my body to turn and look at Mary and Machiavelli, who were mincing their way through the damage, looking a little distraught. Machiavelli undid his outer coat-tunic-thing and handed it to me. I felt a little bad, considering this was the second set of his clothes that I had ruined. I wrapped the garment around me, feeling all my muscles protest at the movement.

"Where is Charlotte?" Mary repeated, looking around more fervently. "We saw Life and Death fighting, and then there was a flash and then everybody was gone. What happened? Where's Charlotte?"

I struggled to my feet, nearly crying out at the pain that lanced through my muscles. I could only imagine what it would really feel like if I didn't have my soul running loose. "Life got her," I said.

"What?" Mary stumbled backwards, almost tripping on an upset cobble. "What do you mean?"

"I mean that Life decided she would take Charlotte, since Death was demanding…" I stopped, unsure how to continue. Death's words hadn't really processed while he was talking, but now that I had a chance to think about them, I realised what he had been saying. *Charlotte* was Death's appointment. The one that he missed. And she was the mortal that Life refused to give up. The whole reason I had been sent back was because of Charlotte. And the whole reason for the future relationship problems between Life and Death, it was because I had stepped in to save that girl when Charlotte was the one meant to do it.

It was my fault. It was all my fault.

I looked at Machiavelli, hoping that he would have the words that would make everything clear. He could explain it to Mary. He could make her understand.

He looked back at me with an ashen complexion. His eyes were wide and glassy and he wobbled in place. Machiavelli no more had the words than I did. He was nothing more than a regular, fragile human who had been pulled into a world that he didn't understand. One that could kill him just as easily as breathing. His famous name and place in history had made me forget that he was mortal. Truly, completely, heartbreakingly mortal. And he had just seen the horrible reality of Life and Death laid before him. What had been a lark before had turned into something out of a nightmare.

I took a deep breath. "Charlotte was Death's appointment," I said before I could stop myself. I had to make them understand. I had to fix this. Which meant—

"No." Mary poked me in the shoulder, the contact painful to my newly reformed person. Her eyes blazed. She took a step closer to me so that she glared up at me with all the hatred she possessed. "You're wrong."

"I saw it myself," I said, holding up my hands. "There's no way that—"

"You're *wrong!*" Mary screamed. The empty square rang with her fury. She clenched her fists at her sides, her belt purse bulging with papers and charcoal, all that was left of her life. "Charlotte *couldn't* be the appointment! She's wouldn't be here if it weren't for *you*. You brought us here. You made us try to search for the person Death was supposed to kill. You did this!"

I stepped back, my foot coming down hard on a jagged edge of stone. I bit back a hiss and took another step back as Mary advanced. "I didn't know!" I said, desperate to explain. I looked between Machiavelli and Mary, hoping that one of them would see the plight, see that I hadn't meant for any of this to happen.

"It doesn't matter," Mary said, the sneer on her face doing a poor job of hiding the contempt in her eyes. "Charlotte didn't deserve this. You didn't deserve her."

"She's not dead," I whispered in protest. Mary's shoulders jerked, but the look she gave me could have easily levelled me flat had it been tangible.

"No, she's in the hands of a madwoman. One who takes pleasure in torturing people, making things as difficult for them as possible. Do you honestly think that is a good thing?" Mary shook her head, not waiting for an answer. Instead, she climbed over the rubble and left the square, vanishing around a corner.

I looked beseechingly at Machiavelli. He swallowed, licking his lips, eyes darting from destroyed garden to upturned street. After a moment, he spoke, the words barely intelligible for being so quiet. "Perhaps we should leave before the city guard and the Medici mercenaries arrive," he said.

I nodded and we two left the square, heading towards Machiavelli's house. I received a few strange glances for my completely inappropriate attire, but no one bothered to speak to us, to stop us and ask questions. They were afraid.

"I'm sorry," I said after we had walked for a few minutes. "I didn't mean for any of this to happen."

Machiavelli nodded, swaying slightly as he walked. He paused and leaned against a wall, a steadying hand resting on the stone. He swallowed again, eyes closed. When he opened them, the fear and emptiness that I saw there struck me worse than the open rage that Mary had shown. "Perhaps… perhaps you shouldn't have gotten me involved in all of this. Perhaps I'm not meant for such things." He took in a deep breath. "I just want to go back to how things used to be."

I reached out, wanting to place a comforting hand on his shoulder. I pulled back a moment later, unable to bear the thought if he flinched away. Instead, we started walking again, moving quickly through the streets so that people wouldn't stare any longer.

I felt a thick sludge settle on my stomach, the emptiness I had pushed aside for perhaps longer than I cared to admit. I was in a time without my usual resources. My friends—people I hadn't realised I missed until just now—were sitting in an office a few thousand miles and several centuries away, laughing together. So what if Yolanda was a rock troll and Agravaine an aggravating air elemental? So what if I worked in marketing for beings of magic? Any of that would be better than being here, where I had messed up so thoroughly that all friendships I had made withered away before my eyes.

Charlotte had been taken and was enduring who knows what horrors. Mary—The Author—hated me for not only stealing her friend away but for the realisation that Charlotte was meant to be dead. Charlotte the Unkillable, brought low by a myopic PR agent. And Machiavelli, whose empty expression was almost worse. I had ripped the rug out from beneath him, making every certainty that he knew questionable.

This was my fault.

Everything was my fault.

And I was never going to be able to fix it.

WISDOM COMES WITH TIME

Once we reached his house, Machiavelli no longer acknowledged my existence. He went about the motions of doing work, pulling out a quill and some ink. For the first time, I saw servants—two people, a man and a woman, who watched the strange behaviours of their master with quiet concern—and did my best to stay out of the way. New clothing, this time much more worn and slightly patched, was procured for me. A bath was heated for Machiavelli, but I made do with a basin in my room and staying out of the way.

After an hour of this confinement, though, knowing that the household would be much happier if I just vanished, I decided that there was little I could do. So I pulled on my shoes and slipped out of the house, walking right past Machiavelli. He just stared vacantly off into space, the poem on the page before him forgotten.

I left to go wander the streets.

The few coins that I had earned during my brief stint as a city guard—and grudgingly returned to me by the Church—had long since been spent on food and wine, the last vestiges of my fortune gone on this afternoon's pity-feast with Charlotte, Mary and Machiavelli. And while I quietly craved the oblivion that I still hoped to find at the bottom of a jug of wine, the thought of interacting with people in a tavern sent chills down my spine. So, broke, tired and ostracised, I wandered through the city gates, promising the guard that I'd be back by dark.

A short while later and I found myself in the middle of a familiar field, a gorge and creek only a few hundred feet away. This was where I had first arrived in 1494. It looked so different, now. Instead of being terrible, it was simply calming and beautiful. Just a field in Italy, somewhere I had always wanted to go. It wasn't the fault of Italy that I was such a cockup.

I looked around for mercenaries, wondering if they would remember me, and found nobody but a few crows in the trees. I wandered to the place where Machiavelli had helped me out of the creek and sat, debating dangling my feet in the water.

"It *is* peaceful here, is it not?"

I looked up, somehow unsurprised to see the figure sitting beside me. Unlike my hand-me-down rags, he still wore that despicably tailored suit, his expression just as calm and sure and arrogant as before. Time smiled at me, tilting his head back to enjoy the sunshine.

"Did you know that all of this would happen?" I

asked, the hardness in my tone surprising even to me. Time chuckled, completely unconcerned by my rancour.

"Dear Cal," he said, shaking his head, "you must be more specific. My mind is not always when you think it should be."

I felt that same wall of rage rising inside me that had Death practically threatening me yesterday. I took a deep breath, reminding myself that just because I was soulless did not mean that I wasn't in control. I was not going to give in to this situation. I grabbed a rock and threw it into the water, watching the resulting ripples and imagining my anger dissipating in much the same way.

"Did you know that my coming here would be the catalyst that starts the problems between Life and Death? Did you know that my friend is meant to die and that I may have sent her somewhere much, much worse? Did you know that I was going to break history?" The words came out in a rush, not nearly so furious as I would have thought. Time said nothing for a moment. I looked at him and saw that he was laughing so hard he had to cover his mouth to keep the sounds from escaping.

"Ah, Cal, how *arrogant* you are," Time spluttered. "Do you think that such an insignificant force as *you* could break history?"

Heat rushed into my face, though whether from embarrassment or anger I couldn't say.

Time shook his head. "I have met only one being

who could change the forces of history and you are decidedly not she."

"So, what," I demanded, "this was all meant to happen?"

Time considered, tilting his head. He rested his weight on his hands behind him, threading his fingers through the grass. "Meant to happen? Is anything *meant* to happen? No, everything that you have done—and everything that everyone else has done—has been a choice. History is made up of choices. Infinite choices. And each choice creates history. There are so many different histories, some of them almost precisely the same, some of them so wildly different you would not believe it possible. Your choices brought you to this history. I had a feeling this might happen, which is why I gave you the advice I did, but I was not certain."

"Shouldn't you *know* these things?" I asked, not understanding. Was he talking about multiple realities or something? Was I meant to do this or not? If my soul weren't missing, I'd have a massive headache.

"I am Time. I am not certainty. I am not the events that happen. I am merely the stream into which they fall and the ripples they create. This point in history created stronger ripples for your being here, which is why I knew to send you here," Time said. His circular logic was bringing back that rage.

"So, yes, you knew—certain or not—that my being here would cause problems," I snapped. "I created the rift between Life and Death."

"There's that arrogance again," Time chuckled. He

took a deep breath. "Life and Death are beings older than even myself. They are supremely powerful in ways that I think you cannot comprehend. You perceive them in a particular way, but that is only part of what they are. The rift between them, the differences that make them fight in such spectacular ways, that has always been there. This particular spot in history may have exacerbated the issue, but it would have always occurred."

"Then why did you even bother sending me here?" I asked. "If their problems were inevitable."

"Because of the possibilities I see before me, many of the possible horrible futures are changed if you are here," Time said. I snorted and pushed my glasses up my nose.

"Weren't you just calling me arrogant a moment ago?" I asked.

"Perhaps," Time said. He flashed me another of those lazy smiles which infuriated me. I pushed the emotion away, the act easier now that I had done it a few times. A cloud covered the sun for a moment, making me shiver.

"Charlotte is going to die," I said once the sunshine had returned.

"Everything dies, Cal," Time replied. For once, he seemed to be taking this seriously, because the expression he wore was solemn, his voice respectful. "You work for Death. You know this."

"Death took my soul," I countered. "So not everything dies."

"Are you sure about that?"

I closed my eyes. I licked my suddenly dry lips. "No."

"In my world, Death is not the end of things. Things do not always flow in a linear fashion. And one choice can spark a thousand, changing the shape of the future," Time said. He held out his hand, a magnetic power rippling over and through it. "You people are far more capable than you think. You have far more agency than I do, than do Life or Death. We are slaves to our nature. You are changeable. Malleable. And more enduring than you know. Do you honestly think that your friend would wish to be the cause of a future that continues from the current trajectory of events?"

I shook my head. I hated Time, just then. He never once denied that all of this was my fault. And yet... "Charlotte is called the Unkillable."

"Why?" Time asked, though I thought perhaps he knew the answer.

"Mary...Charlotte's friend, says it's because it is impossible to kill someone who works so far into the shadows that no one even remembers her." There was a pause after I spoke where my chest filled. I let out a sob, the reality of the situation facing me. I didn't want Charlotte to die. I didn't want anyone to die. But, like Time said, I worked for Death and couldn't deny the inevitability.

"Or is it that it is impossible to kill someone that is never forgotten," Time said.

I laughed, the sound coming through my tears as a strangled croak. "I think Charlotte would like that."

Time inclined his head, smiling lazily once again.

He leaned over and touched the surface of the water, seemingly fascinated by the way the drops came together on his fingers. Then, still leaning over, he twisted his head to look up at me.

"I have to fix this, don't I?" I asked.

"It is a choice you must make, but yes," Time agreed. He straightened, cupping some water in his hand. He tilted it over and watched the drops fall out.

"How am I meant to do that?" I asked. That familiar fear I felt when doing something I usually thought was impossible, was nowhere to be seen. The rage that I had been pushing back was gone, too. So was my tiredness. All of it waited behind that veil in my mind. All that was left was an empty feeling in my stomach that I knew needed to be fixed.

"You were hired by Death because you knew how to communicate with people," Time said. He turned and fixed me in his stare, something wild and untamed there. "So go communicate."

Then, in true Time fashion, he was gone.

"Sometimes," I said, speaking to a crow watching my from across the bank, "I really hate my job."

The crow cawed. I chuckled, the act enough to lighten that pit in my stomach.

"Yeah," I agreed. "Sometimes I really like it, too."

With that, I pushed myself to my feet, took a deep breath, and turned back towards the direction of Florence. The sun was starting to set, painting the sky in shades of colours that were spectacular to behold. Even unable to feel everything as strongly as I normally did, I knew that this was a sight I would never forget. It held beauty, but more than that, it held a promise of a future.

I pulled out my phone and took a picture.

I started walking towards town, thinking of ways to go about finding Life, and therefore Charlotte.

And when I passed some familiar looking men on horseback, I didn't break stride once. I just started running, knowing full well that they would chase me. I had things to do and no Medici-bought mercenaries were going to get in my way.

TIME OF OUR LIVES

When I burst into Machiavelli's house, he had just sat down to dinner and was raising a bite of chicken to his mouth with a trembling hand. At my entrance, he cursed, dropped the strange two-pronged fork, stared, then sank back into his seat.

"Do you never do anything quietly?" Machiavelli asked after a moment. I sat in the chair beside him, smiling gratefully when a plate was placed before me, though the servant looked very much like she hated me. I dug in gratefully, figuring that it was better to be well-fed than walk into potential—okay, definite—danger on an empty stomach.

"I'm a very quiet person," I protested.

Machiavelli shook his head and poured me a cup of wine, his hands still shaking. He put the jug down as soon as he realised I saw his tremor. I didn't say anything, instead choosing to sip at the wine. "You come into my life being chased by mercenaries. Almost immediately, you insult a woman who could flatten you with a single touch, manage to infuriate the Medici —who are both wealthy and powerful, not including your revelation that they are indeed vampiric—goad Death into making a foolish mistake, stage a robbery, get us arrested, then stand between Life and Death. And yet you have the gall to claim that you are a quiet person?"

I couldn't quite tell whether he was joking or being perfectly serious. Given the shaky state of his hands, I assumed the latter. I took a deep breath and set down my wine and my fork. "Okay, Niccolo, let me see if I can lay things out clearly. You think that being awoken to the state of the world was not a kindness. You think that being made aware of things like vampires and half-giantesses and Life and Death, that it was all too cruel for a normal, regular human, no?"

Machiavelli's eyes were suddenly glued to his plate. He said nothing.

"Yep, thought so. Well, let me tell you something; I *was* you. I was a perfectly ordinary person, on my way to a dinner, when I met Death," I said. He lifted his head and scoffed, staring at me as though I were completely insane.

"You were a person in an age where you can speak with another person across the globe with only a tiny piece of metal in your hand! You could travel places faster than any of my peers could possibly comprehend! You had impossibilities at your disposal and yet you tell me that you were *ordinary?*" Machiavelli clapped his mouth shut, alarmed at his outburst. I pulled off my glasses, cleaned them, then perched them back on my nose.

"Yeah, I was perfectly ordinary. Just because those things are impossible now doesn't mean that they are in the future. And even with those things being commonplace, that doesn't mean I was anything special. I wasn't Superman."

"Super-what?" He hunched his shoulders as though I was about to tell him more about the magical world in which we really lived. His eyes were wide, his fingers pulling at the seams of his tunic, his leg jumping up and down beneath the table.

I waved my hand. "Never mind. The point is, had you been born in a different time, it wouldn't change a thing. You and I? We're alike. Human. Perfectly, completely, normal humans. The Elsewhere? The supernatural? Magic? All of that was completely incomprehensible to me. But then I met Death and he offered me a job. You know what? I took it."

"And there you and I differ," Machiavelli said, his eyes once more fixed on his plate.

"Not a bit. Do you know why? Because you came along with me when I went to speak with the Medici. You didn't throw me under the proverbial bus—sorry, cart—when I accidentally insulted Charlotte in the pub and had a giant sword pointed at my neck. You willingly went with me to plan with Charlotte and Mary and you, too, met Death. Talked with him. You and I, we were both offered a chance at taking part in some of the most magnificent things the world has to offer. And it's terrifying."

"I think that is the only thing of sense you have said," Machiavelli murmured. He took a deep breath, sinking further into his chair. I sat back, too.

"You know what else it is?" I asked quietly. Machiavelli flicked his eyes up. "It's amazing."

"*Vampires*, Cal!" he spluttered. "Tatzelwurms! Beings so powerful I can't even comprehend! How is any of that 'amazing'?"

I pulled out my phone and showed him the picture I had snapped of the Italian countryside. "See this? To you, this is commonplace. Normal. The standard landscape. But to me, it's a beautiful picture. It shows me a place I've always wanted to visit. I've travelled through *time* and I get to meet people like you. People like Charlotte. Even Mary, though I'm fairly certain she wants me skinned alive. But the point is, it's something that should be impossible, but it isn't. It's magical. Beautiful. It happens every day. That's what learning about this world is like. It's taking life and turning it into art. It's looking at a painting and seeing something wonderful in the ordinary. It's…it's figuring out a puzzle and seeing the stars. Amazing."

"I…I see still only the fear," Machiavelli replied, voice quiet. He lifted his shoulders and looked at me, helpless. "These beings can tear me to pieces without a second thought."

"Do you know that vampires have really poor sense in fashion?" I asked. Machiavelli gaped at me. "It's true. They can't look at themselves in a mirror, so they have to just sort of guess what looks right. And they could get other people to help them, but other vampires are petty, so they don't always help. If you can appeal to their vanity, you've won that war. And that Tatzel-wurm? You were the only one who figured out that it liked being scratched behind its ears, like a cat."

Machiavelli hunched his shoulders. "It had the head of a cat; it was not so difficult to comprehend."

"See? I wouldn't have thought of that," I said. "I would have just kept yelling at the thing. And Life and Death? Okay, yeah, they're completely terrifying. But Life is far from immune to flattery. And Death loves a good puzzle…All of this that you've seen in the last few days, it always existed. You just didn't see it. It's okay. But do you really *want* to go back to how things were, knowing what wonders lie just within your grasp?"

Machiavelli said nothing. He continued to stare at his plate, taking in steady breaths like he was counting the beats. He closed his eyes. "Did you know that I write poetry?"

"No," I said, though it didn't surprise me. I had seen the pieces of paper he scrawled on.

"Poetry and plays. It is my art. I am no Botticelli, but I have the means to contribute in that way. To contribute to the higher thought of mankind. But when I think of all of the wondrous and terrible things out there that I could never have grasped, not even in my most outrageous poems? It is…difficult. No," he said, looking up at me. "It is far better to understand your world than continue in ignorance."

I nodded. I took another drink of wine and bite of

food. "Okay," I said. "Now with that answer in mind, I'm going to ask for one more favour."

Machiavelli scoffed, but there was a smile at the corners of his mouth. "I am unsurprised by that," he said. "What, do you wish for me to go with you and fight a dragon? Perhaps slay a Titan?"

"Ah, no. Dragons are super scary and really awesome. Or so I've heard; I haven't actually met one," I said. "No, I need your help to go rescue Charlotte."

This statement brought about a coughing fit that took almost a whole minute to subside. Machiavelli slammed his hand against his chest, eyes wide and staring at me. "Are you *insane*?" he demanded.

"Probably." I shrugged. "But Charlotte is my friend and I don't really want to leave her in Life's grasp for any longer than necessary."

"And, what, will you just deliver her to Death? Or had you forgotten that he desires her as well?" Machiavelli said. I shook my head, an idea springing to mind.

"Actually," I said. "I have a thought about how to avoid that. About how to keep Charlotte alive and well and out of the hands of either Life or Death."

He took a deep breath and sat back in his chair, staring up at the ceiling. "Your previous ideas have not gone particularly well, Cal. Perhaps it is better this way. Perhaps Life will tire of Charlotte and leave her be. Perhaps Death will prevail without our assistance. Are you certain about this? About standing before two of the most powerful beings ever imagined, and defying them?"

I explained my idea. After I was finished, he nodded. Took a bite of his food. Chewed slowly. Then, he turned and stared at me for a minute, expression solemn. After a few more moments of consideration, he allowed a grudging nod.

"It is possible."

"It's more than possible," I countered.

"They will be furious," Machiavelli pointed out.

"I know. But what fun is it being human if you don't get to make really stupid decisions every now and again?"

"I was right," Machiavelli said, smiling. He ran a hand through his hair and heaved a sigh. "You *are* insane."

MY PLAN WOULDN'T WORK without Mary, so Machiavelli and I scoured Florence to find her. I asked around at the town squares, seeing if any of the local gossip could direct me to a slightly crazy and very angry woman with quills and parchment. It took a little longer to find her, even with that specific description, but in the end, she was in the only possible place: the library. Actually, given that the libraries of the time were run by monks or owned by extremely wealthy people who had no intent on sharing them with anybody, Mary was pacing angrily outside of a privately owned library that Machiavelli knew.

She rounded on us before we had a chance to call

her name. "Can you believe that these buffoons refuse to acknowledge that I am a writer and perfectly capable of reading these books, just because I am a woman?"

I shrugged, wishing I had some pockets to shove my hands into. "I mean, to be fair, Niccolo here seems to be the only enlightened one of the lot, so…yes?"

"You're an idiot and I hate you," Mary sniffed in reply. She lifted her chin and folded her arms. "What are you doing here? Come to acknowledge what an insufferable piece of—"

"Yes, it was all my fault," I said, holding up my hand to stop her before she could start a long-winded rant about how terrible I was as a person. I really didn't need that right then. "I messed up. Epically. And Charlotte is suffering for it. I'm sorry, Mary. Really. I didn't mean for any of this to happen."

Mary glanced at Machiavelli, narrowing her eyes. "And, what, you accept his apology just like that?" she demanded.

"It was rather more dramatic an apology than that, but his arguments do have their merit," Machiavelli said. He calmly brushed some dirt from his clothes before stepping forwards and holding his hands out to Mary. "I believe that he is sincere in his apologies. He also has some interesting ideas about how to save your friend."

Mary whirled to stare at me, hands clenched into fists at her side. "You know how to save Charlotte? From *both* of those…those…"

I answered before Mary could come up with an

appropriate term to describe Life and Death. Though, there was nothing that quite really managed to do such a thing accurately. Still, I could think of more than a few terms that would be close enough. "Yeah," I said, shuffling my feet. "I have an idea."

At Mary's sceptical brow, I explained my idea. She had much the same reaction that Machiavelli did; she was quiet for a moment, looked back at the library, fiddled with her pouch of writing supplies, then sighed and nodded. "It is possible."

"But...?" I prompted.

Mary threw her hands up. "There are so many ways this could go wrong! We have to get close enough to Charlotte to tell her the idea, then you have to actually do it—do you even know how?"

"Well, no, but I figured you could tell me." I smiled sheepishly. Mary let out a roar of frustration, drawing an angry look from a monk who was watching us through the leaded glass window. I waved, smiling. He pulled back.

"Look, I think this is our best option, okay? If you have another idea, then feel free to let me know," I said.

"No, this is the only idea I've got," she huffed. After a few moments, she threw her head back and heaved a sigh. "Fine! Fine, I'll help you! That doesn't mean I'm not angry, but I'll help you. Now pay attention..."

Mary explained to me, in many florid and far from uncertain terms, precisely what to do, how it could go badly, what was going to happen to me if I failed, and also why I was an idiot. But she did help me. Nearly an hour later, we were all three of us solid on the plan, except for one small problem.

"Do you even know where Charlotte is?" Mary asked, folding her arms.

"I have an idea about that, too," I said, pushing myself to my feet from where I had been sitting on the base of a statue while Mary paced and lectured. "But I'll need some help on that front."

"Oh?" Machiavelli asked, quirking a brow. He stretched and folded his arms, too. "You don't know precisely?"

"Ah…no. But I can find out pretty quickly. I just need some money and the busiest tavern in the city," I said.

"That's it?" Machiavelli asked, looking suspicious. Mary mirrored his expression and cocked a hip, a move so fundamentally female that it startled me for a moment.

"That's it," I replied. "Someone—a really *annoying* someone—recently reminded me that I was hired by Death for a reason. That reason is my ability to communicate with people."

Mary snorted. She stepped away from the library, much to the pleasure of the slightly-angry man I saw still staring at us from the window. Mary shoved her hand into a small pouch at her belt and pulled out three shining golden coins. "Oh, I'll *gladly* pay to see this debacle."

"Indeed, it does seem unlikely," Machiavelli agreed. I huffed and snatched the coins from Mary's hand, gesturing for them to lead the way. Machiavelli smothered a laugh before heading deeper into Florence.

We found ourselves at a tavern in what I would call the worker's part of the city. The people here wore the same sorts of clothes as everyone else I had seen thus far, but it was more worn, more well-used. The people themselves had the same sort of look. The two barmaids serving the tavern looked harried and tired. The diehard drunks over in the corner had that look of desperation about them. The rest of the crowd, though, looked like good, solid people who doggedly worked their way through life.

I slipped two of the coins into my own belt pouch, strode confidently to the wall of barrels with various sorts of alcohols inside and ordered a beer. The barkeep didn't even look at me before putting down a tankard of the amber liquid. I wasn't really a beer guy, but this—much like the wine—was something unearthly. It was rich, foamy, had flavours I couldn't even begin to identify and was strong enough to stick a knife straight up.

I was really beginning to enjoy the beverage selection from this time.

"A round for the whole place," I shouted, putting down the golden coin.

This did make the barkeep look up. He exchanged a glance with one of the barmaids, who blinked in shock, then took the coin before I could pull it away. This was met with a cheer by those people nearest me. They held out their cups and their tankards and before I could even finish my beer, I was sitting at a table with the loudest and friendliest of the bunch, laughing over stories of how I managed to get that coin—swiped it from a writer, I said, to which they joked that no writer ever made that much money. Mary glowered at me from the corner. Two stories in and I was enjoying a general camaraderie with these people. It felt good to be talking with people. To be sharing their stories, to be communicating. I offered a story of my own about my job, though this was changed slightly to make sense for the time. This led to a discussion of professions in the group, which led to a general argument about the future of Florence and eventually ended with a debate on the merit of sheep farming.

Not an hour later and I had the information I needed. With another loud cheer, I paid for one more round of drinks with one of my two remaining coins, waved as though I were drunker than I was, and staggered out of the tavern. A few moments later, Machiavelli and Mary came up to me just as I was brushing off my clothes.

"Your approach to gathering information was...to buy alcohol for everyone?" Machiavelli asked, seeming to be genuinely curious.

"The people with all the money may seem like they know everything and have all the control, but it's the other people—those people—who really control things. Win the populace over, win over the world. Or something like that," I said, wincing at my minced words. Machiavelli furrowed his brows for a moment before an interested gleam shone in his eyes.

Well, great. I hoped I hadn't just inspired some Machiavellian idea. No, well, pun intended.

"Some great communicator," Mary snorted.

"Yes, well, what happens when you buy beer for everybody is that they tell you all of the interesting things going on in the hopes that you will buy them more beer. You are suddenly the most interesting and powerful person in the room," I said. "And what they told me is that something is going on at a camp just outside the city. Something about the mercenaries growing in number and making a whole lot of noise."

Machiavelli shook his head. "I do not see how that helps us."

I grimaced, thinking of my last experience with such things. "Life invariably starts a sort of...party, I guess, wherever she stays for more than a few hours at a time. I'd say that if she's been hanging around, it's where all of the activity and energy and, well, life, is happening. So I asked about that. And it's happening in the mercenary camp."

Mary glared at me, her chin jutted out stubbornly. Machiavelli frowned, but did not say anything. I waited. Finally, Mary huffed. "Is it alright if I hate that you make sense right now?"

"Sure," I said.

"Good." Mary didn't wait for anything else, she just started stalking off in the direction of the city gates. It was well beyond dark at this point and I had no doubt we would catch flack from the city guard about trying to leave so late, but I would not for anything stand in

Mary's way just then. So I didn't. Machiavelli gave another long-suffering sigh and followed after her.

"This is going to end badly," he said quietly to me.

"Pessimist," I quipped. Unfortunately, I had a feeling that he was right. My plan hinged on a lot and I wasn't certain that it would work. Still, it was worth a shot. Now, I just had to go crash Life's party. This would be fun.

Finding Life's party was, surprisingly, quite easy. I would have figured that she wouldn't want to be found, given that Death was annoyed with her, we were annoyed with her and a whole lot of other people were running around scared. But, then, Life had never been one to hide. She was always front and centre, ready for whatever attention would be thrown her way. So finding the party wasn't the problem.

The problem was crashing it.

The mercenaries—there were maybe about a hundred or so of them—had set up camp a little ways from the city, their tents gathered together into their own little community. The ground had been churned up from days' worth of walking around and the whole place was nowhere near as nice or clean as Florence itself. The closer we got to the city, the stronger the feeling was that this was a very, very bad idea.

"You there," a voice called out, making the three of

us stiffen and freeze in our tracks. I turned and saw a familiar face, one that was leering and looking far too pleased to see me. "I thought I recognised you. You were that little fool we chased a few days ago."

"Ah, yes, well," I said, eloquent as ever.

"And now you've come to play," the man sneered. He pulled out a longish sword, fitted it into a two-handed grip and looked extremely pleased with himself. "What fun."

"Actually, I'm looking for someone—"I started to say, but the mercenary lifted his sword to my throat. I lifted my hands and rolled my eyes dramatically at Mary, who snickered.

"Actually, you three are coming with me. It's about time we had some new meat for our games."

It was difficult to argue with a sword at your back, even with my inability to die. I didn't want either Mary or Machiavelli to get hurt and, in all likelihood, this mercenary was going to take us precisely where we wanted to go. Though, the sound of "games" did not appeal.

We were marched through the camp, the centre of which was muddier and more churned up than the outskirts. By the time we reached the other side and were once again on firm ground, we were splattered with mud. Mine was mostly from tripping and nearly falling on my face every time that stupid oaf poked me in the back with his sword. I think the mercenary did it on purpose. All I knew was that my leather boots felt sodden and sludgy and my glasses were spotted with tiny flecks of mud. I quickly stopped worrying about my footwear, though, when I saw what awaited us.

"Charlotte," Mary breathed, though she had enough sense to keep the word quiet. Even Machiavelli let out a gasp of surprise. I, on the other hand, felt a lump in my stomach. This was, unfortunately, what I had feared.

Charlotte was in the middle of a ring made up of torches, surrounded by mercenaries, all clapping and yelling. She had her sword drawn, but her left arm was cut and she was having a hard time holding the massive greatsword with one arm out of commission. Charlotte's opponents were two warriors—there was no other word for it—who were wearing armour. And by armour, I mean real, honest-to-goodness, I saw it in a museum armour. None of this boiled leather nonsense for them. No, they wore the plate armour of paintings, with an articulated arm brace and gauntlets. Their helmets alone would have been enough to help them be a match for Charlotte, but they also wielded weapons. One had a sword—smaller than Charlotte's, but nimbler—and the other some sort of pike.

Charlotte was outnumbered and outgunned…er outsworded? What was worse, though was that this was obviously not her first fight. She had a black eye already blossoming into beautiful colour, a slice on her left ear, and the hunched shoulders of exhaustion. Life was using Charlotte as a gladiator, doing her best to get as much enjoyment out of her champion as she could.

I spotted Life sitting in an ornately carved wooden chair with her legs thrown over one arm, her head leaning casually back, a goblet of wine dangling from her fingers. She kicked her feet lazily, as if she were doing little more than enjoying a play on a summer's afternoon. Her eyes, though, followed the movements of Charlotte and the other fighters with the eagerness of a cat. The mercenaries standing around the combatants in a wide ring were too eager, too excited, too aggressive. They shouted violently at every movement. They screamed when Charlotte scored a hit and stamped their feet and rattled their weapons when she took one. They were being augmented by Life's powers and I could see that she was getting a kick out of all the, well, life being displayed before her.

Essentially, things were not going well.

The mercenary at our backs pushed us forwards so that Mary, Machiavelli and I stumbled through the outer ring of people. The three fighters paused for a moment, wavering as we tripped into the ring.

Silence descended. Life rose to her feet and looked down at us, fury plain on her stunning features. "You dare to come here," she hissed.

I pushed myself off the ground and wiped my hands free of dirt and mud as best I could. I pulled off my glasses and cleaned them on the least dirty part of my shirt, though it didn't help much. Mary and Machiavelli stood as well, flanking me so that we three faced Life. I could see her power moving towards us like a wave. Machiavelli sucked in a breath as it hit us, but he did not falter. Mary swayed a bit, but eventually she straightened, too, eyes blazing.

"Yeah, we dare. You took something that doesn't belong to you," I said once I was certain my companions could stand up to Life's onslaught. They wouldn't be able to do so for long, but I had a hope that it would be long enough for us to put our plan into action. Only, the biggest part of our plan was currently standing with her sword pointed into the ground, breathing heavily and bleeding from multiple cuts.

Life seemed to grow taller, her anger making her expansive. "And you think she belongs to *you*? Or are you just the messenger for my husband, fool that he is."

I shook my head. "Charlotte belongs to herself. *All* your champions belong to themselves. You don't get to meddle like this."

Life tossed her head, letting out a single bark of laughter. "Oh? I do not get to meddle in my own affairs, in my own domain? These beings are alive, are they not? My champions *live,* do they not? Death can have the dead, but he needs to stay out of my affairs!"

I winced, my ears starting to ring at the sound of Life's voice in my ears. Beside me, Machiavelli shifted his stance so he would be less likely to wobble. Mary reached out and rested a hand on my arm, gathering as much support as she could. "I am not here on behalf of Death. Not right now. And just because they live does not mean that you can do whatever you want. That's not how this is meant to be."

"And how would you know, mortal?" Life asked. She took a threatening step towards me. "You know *nothing* of how things are meant to be."

"Maybe." I shrugged. "But I know that this is wrong. You are torturing your so-called 'champion' into fighting for you because she refused to fight you in the first place. Isn't life about choice? Isn't it about choosing which direction you go, even if it is difficult? Yeah, you maybe get to throw obstacles in our way, but we mortals get to decide how to live."

Life clenched her fists and her figure blazed blindingly for a moment. "Insolent mortal!" Life screamed. Mary and Machiavelli—and pretty much everybody else in the clearing—fell to the ground, their eyes squeezed shut and their hands clasped over their ears. I was pushed back a few steps, but I refused to look away or to cover my ears. A moment later and the shrill sound faded, leaving Life glaring at me, chest heaving to control her anger.

"Fine," she snapped. "I will make you a deal. You best my champion in a duel and I will release her to you."

"Great," I said. "Agreed."

"To the death, then," Life said, grinning widely.

And this is why you always get agreements in writing before saying yes to something, Cal, I scolded myself.

Life clapped her hands and a moment later, the fighting ring was cleared. Charlotte stood there with her sword, frowning at me like a dog who got sprayed by a skunk. Mary and Machiavelli were standing off to one side, eyes wide, but arms held tightly by Charlotte's two previous opponents. Life clapped her hands again. "Begin."

Charlotte wasted no time in rushing for me, her sword held high. I yelped and dove to the side. "You idiot!" Charlotte snapped, swiping the blade by my head. I had a feeling she missed on purpose. Or, at least, I hoped so. "What did you think you were doing, coming here?"

"Rescuing you?" I asked, jumping aside again. I looked around and saw a discarded pike on the ground. I picked it up and felt the tip of Charlotte's blade dig into my shoulder. It wasn't a deep wound, or even a very painful one, but I felt it. "Hey!" I protested.

"Well, try harder," Charlotte said. She advanced towards me again, slower, as though the pike I held was actually dangerous. "What did you think you were going to do, hmm, Cal? Waltz in here and demand my freedom? Life is not a kind mistress."

"Oh, no, I knew that," I said. "And now we're in a fight to the death. Only I can't die and you can whoop my tail without even trying. So we're going to end up at a standstill."

"I think I'd like to try killing you," Charlotte said. As if to prove her point, she lunged towards me and sank the weapon into my hip. I yelped, this time louder, and twisted away. It must have hit an artery or something, because my body started to repair itself, just as it did with all fatal wounds these days. "Darn," Charlotte said drily.

"Will you *stop* that?" I grumbled. "I have a plan!"

"You brought my friends here to get hurt! To die! Or worse," Charlotte retorted. She cast a slightly anxious look towards Mary and Machiavelli. "Cal, you're worse than an idiot."

"Don't worry," I said, trying to be cheerful as I swung the pike around haphazardly. "They're here to help. Mary brought the Eye of Carteria."

Charlotte faltered, which made me accidentally prod her already-wounded arm with the pike. I pulled back as soon as I could manage—man, was I out of shape—and winced an apology. Charlotte touched her throat with her wounded hand and widened her eyes when she realised that the Eye was not there.

"How—"Charlotte asked. "I thought after the vault that I—"

"Mary held onto it after you showed it to us in the tavern. Look, I know that you think bringing them here was a bad idea. And maybe it was, but it was important that they come, okay?" I said, breathing hard and pretending to rest on my pike.

Charlotte swung her sword in my direction again, the metal hitting the wooden shaft and chipping it. "They cannot do anything. She—"

"Oh, relax, will you? They're not going to go up against Life," I snapped. Charlotte narrowed her eyes and swung her sword at my head again. "Mary's going to provide distraction. And Niccolo… well, he's here to help however he can."

"I cannot use the Eye of Carteria," Charlotte said. Her eyes darted to where Life was watching our exchange, looking annoyed. Obviously we weren't trying hard enough to kill one another. "It would… I'm not strong enough for that."

"I think you are," I said, "but I didn't have Mary bring the Eye for you. I had her bring it to be used *on* you."

Charlotte took two massive steps towards me and locked my pike in the crosspiece of her sword. I winced, my arms shaking as I tried to hold her back. "What?" Charlotte asked, voice quiet and eyes wide. "What are you saying?"

"Look, you were supposedly meant to die back in the square. *You* were the appointment Death missed and it's all my fault. It's my fault that you got brought here to be Life's little gladiator. Now both of them want you and there's only one thing I can do about it that doesn't involve actually killing you." I leaned closer, baring my teeth in what I hoped looked to Life like a ferocious snarl. "Take you out of play."

"The Eye of Carteria—"

"Contains. It doesn't kill. You wouldn't be 'alive' persee for Life to take advantage of. You wouldn't be dead. You'd be like me…in a sort of stasis. You could be summoned by the Eye. You'd be bound to it. Not alive or dead. No Death, no Life." I spoke these words as quickly as I could manage.

I felt the weight Charlotte was pushing down on me lessen. My pike slid an inch or two along her blade. Charlotte furrowed her brows, frowning as she considered my words. Behind us, Life let out an angry hiss.

"Why aren't you fighting properly?" she demanded. I swallowed, knowing that our few moments of conversation were at an end.

I pushed back against Charlotte, surprised at the lack of resistance. Charlotte stumbled back a few feet, her sword dragging. I lowered the pike, trying to pretend like I was looking for the best place to strike. I took a tentative step forwards, my eyes darting to gauge Life's expression, her level of anger. Charlotte shook off the shock my words had given her and threw herself back into the fight with a desperation I doubted I would ever be able to match. Charlotte was a fighter, through and through. I was really good with social media, but not so good in a fight.

"What are the consequences?" Charlotte asked, swinging her sword high then low.

"I don't know. We didn't have time for research," I said, doing my best to parry her blows. "But we have to act *now*."

"Okay," Charlotte said, eyes locking with mine. She blinked a drop of blood out of her eyes. "Okay. What do I have to do?"

"Get me close to Mary," I said. "I'll do the rest."

"Cal, you can't use the Eye," Charlotte said, looking alarmed. "You'll—"

"Die?" I replied with as much of a grin as I dared. She rolled her eyes then pushed me back with a massive shove. I tripped over my feet, dropped the pike, fell, rolled, and ended up on my back looking right up into Mary's furious eyes.

"Hi," I said. "Where—"

"Belt pouch by the scrolls," Mary whispered. The warrior holding her eyed her suspiciously as she spoke, but he was too slow to stop me from reaching up and pulling the pouch open. I reached into the bag and grabbed the Eye. I rolled to my feet and turned to face Charlotte. "Stop him!" Life yelled, standing and furious. She pointed at me, but it was too late. I had already held the Eye up and was chanting the words that Mary had supplied to me.

The hand I held the amulet in started to burn blue with power. I could feel the artefact fighting my control, pumping back seemingly endless amounts of power into my body as I tried to claim its power. It would most definitely have killed me, under different circumstances. As it was, I felt fire burning through my blood, scorching my veins and setting my heart ablaze. My lungs felt like they were being crushed by an impossible weight. Still I forced the words out of my mouth and focused my will on Charlotte.

Unfortunately, I had strayed too close to the other mercenaries. They obeyed Life's command, though doing so would surely kill them with the residual magic flowing through me. The warrior holding Mary's arm released her and swung his sword towards me. He didn't hit me properly, but the metal did make contact with the Eye of Carteria in my hand. Power from the amulet surged through this new connection, leaping into the mercenary. He screamed, fire burning him down to his plate armour in less than a minute. And then, it did the unthinkable. It leaped to the closest person, trying to escape the control I was forcing on it.

Mary let out a horrified shriek as the power of the amulet furiously tried to consume her, too. I chanted at the top of my voice, now, but it was no good. I wouldn't be able to exert my will over the Eye before it consumed Mary.

Charlotte let out a roar, the bellow of a giant backed by battle magic, and moved faster than I would have thought possible. She threw herself into the path of the power eating Mary. I tried to force the amulet to contain her, to trap her, not to kill her, but I hadn't yet gained control. Instead of being saved, I watched as Charlotte was killed by the very thing I thought would help her.

She, too, burned until there was nothing left but ashes and her sword. I managed to grab onto the hand with the amulet with my other hand and force it down, pushing the power back into the Eye, though it probably killed me several times over. The power dissipated, then was gone.

And so was Charlotte the Unkillable.

"You," Life snarled. She crossed the ring and stopped before me, quivering with barely suppressed rage. I tried to catch my breath as she looked down at me, but the flutter of fear that I had felt despite my soulless state was growing. I sucked in one last breath as Life reached down and wrapped her hand around my throat.

"Cal!" Machiavelli called out. I tried to turn and stop him from doing something stupid, but Life was already lifting me into the air. Her hand scorched my skin where it touched, but no matter how much I tried to struggle, there was neither relief nor end. My inability to die was no boon; it was a curse that continued to put me into a realm of pain and horror the likes of which I never would have been able to imagine.

I'd had nightmares about this sort of situation for months after the last bout with being unable to die. I was still terrified of pain. And now, it seemed that those fears were justified. I closed my eyes and tried not to whimper.

Life lifted me until my legs dangled off the ground. She held me at eye level and bored her gaze into me. "You will pay for what you have done."

"Gragklack," was may natural response.

"Put him down."

The voice filled the air, silky and cold. There was a slight relief as some of Life's power was pushed aside. I flicked my eyes—now desperately painful and strained—over my shoulder and saw Death approaching, his own expression just as furious as Life's.

"No!" Life said, her lips twisted in disgust. "You did this! *You* sent him here to take my champion. You have ruined everything! Were you too much of a coward to do it yourself?"

"I did not send him," Death said. He walked forwards, his steps calm and measured, his expression calculated. He stopped a good ten feet from where Life held me dangling in the air and clasped his wrists behind his back, the picture of serene patience. If serene patience were fond of gloating. "You know as well as I that you could not keep your champion. She was set upon her path long ago."

Life threw me down to the ground where my spine cracked and I wheezed in a breath. The injuries around my neck were healing and I felt my back knit itself together again. My eyes were stuck on the sky as I tried to gain control of myself once more, but it did not stop me from hearing the screams as the mercenaries all realised what was happening and fled. The other sounds were the resulting thuds of two colossuses colliding.

"Cal!" Machiavelli knelt on the ground, shaking my shoulder. "You have to do something!"

"Grrrglll," I wheezed. I sucked in a deep breath. The ground shook and dirt flew. Mary screamed, the sound enough to compel me into motion. I rolled onto my side and, with the help of Machiavelli, stood. What faced me was even worse than seeing Charlotte battling for her life and freedom.

Life and Death were trading blows, each glaring at the other with unabashed hatred. Life threw a hit to Death's head and he jabbed her in the stomach. She staggered back, only to gather her power in her palms and throw it at Death. He dodged, but the fleeing mercenary behind him was not so lucky. The man immediately began giggling so loudly that he couldn't draw in a proper breath. The grass and other plants around him began to grow so swiftly that they tangled his feet. He suffocated on laughter, trying to tear the vegetation from his limbs. Death's power was equally as destructive, draining the people and earth it encountered until there was nothing left but dust.

If they continued like this, not just Florence would be in danger. They would tear the world apart.

"Mary, I'm so sorry," I said. "Niccolo, I wish you all the best." Then, I pushed them both aside and ran to stand between Life and Death. No plan. No magical artefact. No weapons. Just me standing against the forces of the universe.

I was the only one who could.

They both slammed into me with enough force to shatter my bones several times over. I let out a cry of pain, unable to keep it in. Then, as I sank to my knees, cradling my arms in my lap, I screamed at the two of them.

"ENOUGH!"

Death paused, looking down at me as though he hadn't realised I was even there. Life planted her feet a few inches away, holding a fighting stance and ready to attack. "What are you *doing*?" I asked, my throat producing little more than a croak.

"It is in my nature to oppose him," Life snarled. Death lifted his chin.

"And I will always be waiting to embrace everything you think you possess," Death replied evenly. They inched forwards, ready to start battling again.

"No!" I glowered up at them. "You're both wrong."

"Oh?" Death asked, raising an eyebrow. He towered over me, wearing an expression of smug certainty. This Death was not the Death that had hired me in the park. This Death was something else entirely: uncontrolled, untamed, uncaring. It didn't matter. I still had to do this. "And what do you think is going on?"

"I think you're too scared to realise how little power you actually have," I said. I straightened as much as I could, but even my body was running beyond exhausted. The darkness beyond the torches seemed to swell forwards, barely kept away by the fire.

"How *little* power?" Life laughed skeptically. She shook her head at me like I was an ignorant child.

"Yeah," I said. "How little power. You think you're so

wonderful because you embody life. Because you exist where people laugh and dance and rage and live. But if there weren't anybody or anything, then where would you be? And you," I said, turning to look at Death. "Sure, every living thing will come your direction in the end, but you don't collect our souls. You don't rule over us after we die. If there weren't anybody or anything, who would you come for? What purpose would *either* of you have if it weren't for us? Us mortals, or even the immortals? The people who inhabit this place and Elsewhere? You have only as much power as *we* give you. And I say that we've had enough!"

Death crouched on the ground to peer into my face. Previously, I had been afraid to ever look too deeply into his eyes. They were nothing but voids, empty and impossibly dark. But now, I stared back and was unafraid. Because all that looked back was me. And Charlotte. Mary. Machiavelli. Yolanda. Agravaine. All of us.

"It is an interesting theory," Death said, tilting his head.

"It's more than a theory. Life here draws her power from the living, but that doesn't mean she gets to control us. And Death draws his power from the dying, but that doesn't mean he gets to decide our death. We do. It's *our* choice. Yeah, some people will die in accidents or from natural causes. Yeah, some people will be oppressed or beaten down so they don't really get a chance to live. But you know what? It's still *ours*. The past. The future. History is made up of our choices. Okay, sure, we mess up. A lot. But we're still making our own choices. You two aren't doing any better than we are; you're just making it worse, really. You seem to have forgotten your place in this grand order of ours."

"Your friend Charlotte was destined to die," Death countered. Life snorted and folded her arms, but she did not argue or fight.

"No," I said. "She *chose* to die to save her friend. It's horrible, and I'm going to miss her, but it's the truth."

"Cal," Mary whispered. I smiled up at her, then turned back to my two charges. They looked down at me with expressions of offended interest and anger. Death watched me like he would a chess game. Life just sneered.

"I was sent here by Time to fix the problems in your relationship. But you know what? I think I was sent here to fix the problems in your relationship with *us*. You have thrived for years off of the fear that we've given you. People are afraid to live just as much as they are afraid to die. But whether we do or not, we don't need you to whisper in our ears. It's our choice. Not yours."

"And what would you have us do?" Life sneered. "Vanish? Leave a void behind?"

"Stop interfering." I swallowed and tried to get my feet beneath me. I failed, but my words kept rising. "Leave us to make our choices. You are not unimportant. Nor will you be gone, vanished. But you have had too direct an involvement and you have forgotten that *we* are the ones who gave you power to begin with."

Death let out a long breath. "You demand a difficult

boon, Cal Thorpe. What right do you have for such a demand?"

I held up the Eye of Carteria, still pristine and shining even after all the magic it had wielded. It seemed so innocuous. Yet it had killed two people and I hadn't even finished accessing its magic. I swallowed down my guilt and shoved it into the faces of Life and Death. "This was created to contain the world of magic to Elsewhere. It was done to keep the two realms separate because their continued involvement was dangerous and destructive. You say that you went to Elsewhere by choice. All I'm asking is that you go back there and remember that choice. You're not better than one another. Life isn't greater than Death, only different. And Death may be inevitable, but only because of Life. We're the ones with the power. So leave us to use it how we will."

Death said nothing for a moment. I searched Life's expression, hoping to see any signs of what she thought, but she turned her face away from me, chin lifted. I looked back to Death, whose expression was as unreadable.

"It is possible you have a point," Death conceded after a few more beats. "Our...roles have been muddied for some time, now."

"What, you want to just *leave*?" Life demanded of her husband. Death stood and held out his hand, dark power shimmering there.

"Cal is right, my love. We are not of this world. We are created by the beings here, fed power by them. That does not give us the right to do more than we ought."

Life looked around, seeing the bloody remains of her party. All the enjoyment, the passion and power, that was gone now. What remained were three tired humans who had stood their ground simply because there was no one else to do so. Mary was shaking. Machiavelli looked as though he had aged in the few hours since our coming here. And I would have been in literal pieces if not for a chance accident of time travel.

"Very well," Life said, taking Death's hand. She looked down her nose at me. "We will restrict our influence to that for which we were meant. But we will not be gone, Calvin Thorpe. Never gone."

I sighed. "I never figured you would be."

Then, with barely a whisper, Death and Life vanished back to the places they belonged, hand in hand. I closed my eyes and let my shoulders slump. The Eye of Carteria fell from my hands and I couldn't find it in me to care. Instead, I tilted my head up to the stars and let out a breath. It was done. There had been a terrible cost. But it was done.

"You know that you haven't really solved anything."

I blinked open my eyes and winced at the brightness of the sun glaring in through the window at me. I turned my head away in disgust, slightly surprised at the fact that my muscles were sore and tired and not made of pudding.

"What happened?" I croaked, my throat dry enough that the sounds were barely audible.

"What happened is you passed out." Machiavelli appeared over me, holding a goblet of something in his hands. I sat up as best I could and took a sip: clear, blessed, sweet water. It occurred to me that I hadn't tasted pure water since arriving in 1494. This was something wonderful to behold, crisp and even slightly cool. I sat up more, taking the last of the water and letting out a groan at the protest of my muscles.

"Passed out?" I asked. Machiavelli nodded. He looked surprisingly well rested, considering what had just happened to us. What…I sank my head back down on the bed, remembering everything clearly. Despite all my efforts, I had failed to save Charlotte. She had still died. And Life and Death were still just as powerful and dangerous as ever, even if they were in Elsewhere. Not to mention they probably now had it out to get me.

"Indeed. Almost as soon as those two left, you fainted. The Author—that is, Mary—has assured me I am to use the term 'passed out' as a more pleasing statement. But whatever you wish to call it, we were a little annoyed that we had to practically carry you back here. Through fields. In the dark. You've been asleep for two days, now."

"Two days!" I sat up swiftly, not thinking of my sore muscles or the splitting headache the movement gave me. I hissed and pressed the heel of my palm to my head. I was a little confused as to why my lack of soul didn't prevent me from feeling this pain. My grief for Charlotte's sacrifice was less than what it should be—in fact, I hardly felt that at all—but I still had a splitting headache and sore muscles after sleeping for two days?

I would rather have felt the grief. It didn't seem fair.

"Indeed," Machiavelli said, smirking slightly. He poured more water from a jug and handed it to me. I sipped this one slowly, my eyes narrowed against the light. "Apparently, being immune to dying does not mean that your body feels no toll from your exertions. Mary was surprised that you did not just dissolve into nothingness, though I gather that was more wishful thinking."

I closed my eyes and barely managed to set the

water aside before my hands started trembling. "I didn't want Charlotte to die," I said.

Machiavelli rested a hand on my shoulder. I opened my eyes and looked up at him. "I know," he said. "And Mary knows, also. It does not mean she does not feel pain, but she understands. I think. She has been downstairs, using up all my paper and ruining my quills, barely sleeping."

"Maybe I should talk to her," I said. Before Machiavelli—or my own mind—could convince me that I was wrong, I swung my legs over the side of the bed and stood. I was wobbly, but I did not fall over. That was good enough for me.

I reached for my old clothes folded on a stool in the corner—that is, my clothes from the future—and shoved my limbs into them automatically. I suppose it would have been better to take the clothes that Machiavelli offered, but it felt good to be back in something familiar, even if it was all I had. I found the remains of my phone in the pouch where I had last left it. The screen had been cracked and no matter what I did, it would not power on. I imagine it had died during my fight with Charlotte. I hoped I wouldn't be needing it, but I slipped it into my pocket in any case. I didn't want to leave behind any of the pictures I had taken. I didn't want to forget.

"You are leaving," Machiavelli said, watching me lace my shoes on. I blinked, startled.

Was that why I wanted to wear my own clothes?

"I suppose I am," I replied. "I've done what I was meant to do. I think. Though I'm not sure that things will have improved between Life and Death in my time."

"I did not think they would. You were very eloquent there, but those two…their natures are firm and unchanging. We mortals may have the ability to choose, but I am not sure they do."

I nodded. Swallowed. Said nothing. "Yeah," I agreed. "But I had to try."

"I know." Machiavelli helped me to stand again and then held the door open for me. I slipped out of the room and went down the stairs to find Mary precisely where Machiavelli said she would be. At my entrance, she paused in her scribblings, ink stains on her fingers and nose, eyes narrowed.

"You," Mary said flatly.

"Hello," I said. "Look…I'm sorry about the way that things went down. I didn't mean for that to happen. I tried to contain the power, but I wasn't fast enough. I wanted to save her, not…you know."

"That doesn't change what happened," Mary said. She lowered the quill to the table and rose. She, too, I noticed was looking differently than she usually did. In fact, she looked more like Charlotte than Mary. She wore men's clothing, the sort that was easy to move in and fight in. Instead of her belt and pouches, she had a satchel on the table, open to reveal some of her scrolls and charcoal. Underneath that lay Charlotte's greatsword, oiled and glistening.

"You can't take her place," I said. "I mean, Charlotte may be gone but that doesn't meant that you have to…"

"Become her?" Mary asked, tilting her head.

"I guess." I shoved my hands into my pockets, a faint smile breaking through once I realised that I had pockets again. Proper pockets.

"I'm not trying to become her. I'm a journalist. A writer. Charlotte was an adventurer. A fighter. An honourable person. But someone has to take the Eye of Carteria to the Library at Sazhem. And after that? Who knows. Maybe there are other dangerous artefacts out there. People whose stories need to be told." Mary lifted her chin defiantly, daring me to challenge her.

"Hard to kill someone who won't be forgotten, isn't it," I said. My shoulders hunched and I shook my head, the image of Charlotte being consumed vibrant in my head. I blinked rapidly and pushed my glasses up my nose, hoping that the scratched lenses would hide some of my distress.

"Cal?" Mary asked, taking a tentative step forwards.

"Though, you're going to have to come up with a different name than The Author," I said, forcing myself to laugh. Mary hesitated then sat back down, nodding. She picked up a quill and ran her fingers over the feather.

"I suppose. I don't know about Mary, though," she said. "It's too…staid."

"I'm sure you'll figure something out." I looked around the little room, hoping to find something to comment on, something to prolong the moment and pretend that I wasn't about to walk away from Mary and Machiavelli and all of the things that had happened between us. There was nothing.

"Take care of yourself, Cal," Machiavelli said after

the silence had stretched on for too long. Mary blinked and eyed me warily.

"You're leaving." It wasn't a question and it wasn't said in disappointment.

"I have to get back to work," I said, shrugging. "And, you know, find my soul."

"Good luck with that," Mary said, though it was plain she was sceptical about the whole thing. "Not being able to die can make you foolish."

"Do you know, I think you might be right?" I asked, this time my laughter genuine. After a moment, Mary joined in, shaking her head. Machiavelli clapped me on the arm.

"Come," he said. "Let us go. The city gates will be unguarded for a few more hours while the authorities try and sort out what has happened these last few days. There have been stories of gods walking the earth, of demons and angels, and people seem to be sporting spectacles more than before. The authorities are quite busy. Too busy to worry about the French, even though our mercenary army has diminished greatly."

I nodded, only half-listening to the words. I waved to Mary with a smile and followed Machiavelli outside. We walked in silence to the gates. I admired Florence, thinking that it would be nice to come here when the world wasn't about to fall apart. It really was beautiful. Artistic. Colourful. Every so often, Machiavelli would look at me. Then he would shake his head and look away.

"You know, the Medici—vampires or not—are going to be around for a while. All of this, the magic and the wonder, it's not going anywhere," I said just as we reached the gates. I stopped and looked at him, framed there by the stones. "You may as well embrace it."

"Somehow, it all seems so much more...terrifying now that I know you are walking away," Machiavelli said. I shook my head and put my hands on his shoulders.

"You'll be fine. Trust me. Just enjoy what you have and don't be afraid of the future," I said. Machiavelli laughed, shaking his head hard enough that he had to hold his cap on with a hand.

"That's the advice you have for me? You come all this way from the future and that is what you offer?" Machiavelli laughed all the harder.

"Well, let's just say that history wasn't my best subject." I hunched my shoulders apologetically. I left Niccolo Machiavelli standing just outside Florence, laughing furiously. It was a sight I wasn't bound to forget anytime soon.

—

Time didn't even wait for me to reach the spot where we had met twice before. He just appeared at my side as I was walking down the road, plain as day for anyone to see. I raised my brows at him.

"Well, did you learn any lessons?" Time asked, smirking. I rolled my eyes.

"Why do I get the feeling that you're mocking me?"

I retorted. Time chuckled and slung an arm around my shoulder.

"Because you are not dumb, Cal Thorpe," Time said. "Now, if you don't mind, I'm in a bit of a hurry. I left someone in the 60s and really must get back there. Besides, I'm sure you have more interesting things to do than stick around and chat with me."

"Wait, what—"I started, but the damage was done. Time touched my forehead and the world went white. When I came to my senses, I was swaying on my feet and feeling extremely woozy. At least I wasn't screaming.

The world around me wasn't the fields and hills outside Florence. There was no birdsong, no spring sunlight. There was, however, a familiar walnut floor and desk, the air filled with the long-missed smell of coffee. This wasn't a theatre, or a city. I was in my office. I was home.

"Cal?" Yolanda asked, standing from the desk where I had left her. Agravaine was at her side, frowning. "You look funny. I thought you were just going to the theatre."

I smiled wanly at my assistant. There was an emptiness in my chest that I rubbed absently. I stopped when I realised what I was doing. The emptiness remained. "Do you know, that's kind of a long story. Why don't you go make some popcorn?"

Yolanda grinned, flashing those extremely white teeth, then bounded off to the office kitchen. Agravaine sighed and sat on the edge of her desk. "Dr. Graveltoes posted more selfies. It's looking like we're going to have to take away his social media privileges entirely. Then there's a summons from the dwarf kingdom of Aggra... Aggrl... Someplace I couldn't pronounce unless I swallowed rocks. They want to have you market the ascension ceremony for their new queen. I told them you were booked for months but..."

I smiled and shook my head, both motions feeling simultaneously natural and artificial. It was good to be home. To see Yolanda and Agravaine. But there was still the weight of my now-broken phone in my pocket and the emptiness that was quickly growing in my chest.

I took a deep breath and pulled out the phone, tossing it on my desk. "Tell you what. You figure out where to get me a new phone around here and I'll let you take on the dwarfs yourself."

Agravaine's frown turned into a full-on scowl. "You have got to be kidding me."

It was good to be home.

NO TIME LIKE THE PRESENT

Two days later, I walked into Death's house, pausing just long enough to notice that it was looking the same as ever: grand, beautiful in an old world kind of way, with enough care taken that it was plain someone lived there. It was stunningly expensive and had a sort of contemplative, melancholy air, as if it breathed. There were no servants, as far as I could tell, but the doors to Death's library swung open for me all the same.

I found Death sitting in a club chair by a roaring fire, a leather-bound book with minuscule text in his hands. He was wearing a tweed suit with patches at the elbows and knees—what amounted to casual clothes for him. Coupled with the slight smile on his lips as he read, Death looked more relaxed than I had ever seen him. Maybe my time in the past had done some good.

Or maybe it hadn't.

"Ah, Cal," Death said, closing his book. He examined me with those empty voids that were his eyes, brows rising slightly. "I see. You've reached that point in time, haven't you?"

"You mean the point where your cousin yanked me backwards to apparently go fulfil some sort of self-fulfilling prophecy or the realities of history or something? Yes, I've reached that point." I paused a moment, wondering whether I was being sarcastic or not. I wasn't quite sure.. "You have a strange family."

Death sighed and massaged his temple. "You have no idea. But you soon will."

"Do I even want to know?" I sank into the club chair opposite Death, not waiting for an invitation. Death watched the movement with something akin to surprise in his gaze.

"Interesting," he said, making a musing hum. "How very interesting indeed."

"What? That I'm not afraid of you anymore?" Again, I wasn't sure whether I was being sarcastic, but the part of me not quite affected by the loss of my soul seemed to think I was genuinely curious. The lack of emotion, the inability to tell what I was feeling, it was getting worse.

Much worse.

"Should you ever have been? After all, inevitability is not despair." Death watched me for a moment. I said nothing, rolling his words around in my head. It made sense, I suppose. But I wasn't here for philosophy.

Death let out a breath and leaned back into the chair. "I don't have your soul, Cal," he said.

"Ah." I frowned, sure I was meant to be feeling

something other than a slight twinge of disappointment. Anger, perhaps. "Do you know where it is?"

"I am afraid not," Death said. "Like its owner, your soul is rather difficult to pin down. And matters of the soul are not my area of expertise. Nor are they Life's. I asked."

"So what do I do now?" I asked. I rubbed the back of my head. "It's been two days since I got back and I think things are getting worse."

"They would," Death said, nodding his head gently. "In the past, you had only been without your soul for a few days. Your emotions were volatile, difficult to control and perhaps not all there. But now, you have been without your soul for many centuries. It may only objectively be a few days, but your soul has travelled through time the long way around. Without a soul, you soon won't feel anything at all. I do not know what will happen after that."

I licked my lips, surprised that they were suddenly dry. "Where do I even start looking?"

"I do not know that, either," Death admitted. Then, he did something that seemed odd, even given my strange flat, emotionless state. He leaned forwards, resting his elbows on his knees, and grinned. "But I know where you can get a temporary soul."

"A...temporary soul?" I asked.

"Indeed." Death chuckled, the sound sending shivers down my spine though I did not know why. "How do you feel about playing poker?"

ACKNOWLEDGMENTS

I would love to thank all of you who have stuck with me through this wild journey thus far. You can expect many more adventures with Cal in the future!

Thanks especially to Fay Lane, whose covers always manage to impress and convey the perfect sentiment for this slightly bizarre, but oh so much fun series.

Thank you also to Michael Evan, who helped to edit this mess into the shenanigans you find now.

A special thanks to Alexzander Christion, who is the original creator of Charlotte. Or, well, who gave a name to her at least.

And, as always, thank you to my dad for listening to me drone on and on about Time and Death and Machiavelli, usually with no context whatsoever.

I hope to see you all in the next adventure!

ABOUT THE AUTHOR

E.G. Stone is an independent author who has been writing, creating and causing vast amounts of trouble since the age of six. Since then, E.G. has improved rather a lot in both the trouble-causing and writing and now spends her time writing fantasy and science fiction. When not writing, she is off musing about the workings of languages, both real and created, or drawing and sewing. E.G. reads voraciously, perhaps to the point of slight-insanity. Weird, nerdy, perhaps a little crazy, she is having a grand old time writing, reading, reviewing, interviewing, and, naturally, continuing her endeavours in causing trouble.